DISCOVERED

A DEVON CHILDS ADVENTURE

Daniel Marc Chant

SEVERED PRESS

HOBART TASMANIA

DISCOVERED

ISBN: 978-1-925711-07-3

For Nathan Drake.

CHAPTER ONE

"Welcome students," the professor said, pacing at the front of the lecture hall. "I am Dr. Devon Childs and I will be your veterinarian professor for your first term here at Whateley College. I have to say, you've made a wonderful choice coming here."

She smiled and looked up at the assembled students. They had intent eager faces, wide eyes. Many were scribbling notes already, even though this was their first lecture and she hadn't said anything important yet. Some of course looked bored already, their chins resting on their hands, eyes staring off into space. Her smile widened and she gave a soft chuckle.

"Now," she said, raising her voice, "You may think that the uses for veterinarian medicine are few and obvious but I'm here to tell you otherwise. I am a veterinarian, true, but I'm also something else. I am a Cryptozoologist. Who can tell me what that is?"

She was met with blank faces. Then a hand hesitantly raised.

"Yes," she said with a smile. She pointed at the student. "You, beside the SLEEPING STUDENT WITH THE STUPID HAT."

The student in question jumped awake with a thump as their head slipped off their hand and slammed into the desk. The rest of the students laughed. The previously sleeping student rubbed their forehead and smiled in embarrassment. The student who had raised their hand grinned at them and turned back to look at Devon.

"A cryptozoologist is a scientist who wanders around trying to prove the existence of unicorns and dragons." The student said confidently. There was a smirk on his face and scorn in his voice.

Devon grinned and began to pace. She shook her head. She'd heard it all before and those attitudes no longer bothered her like they once had.

"That is indeed a common misconception," she said, her confidence building as she started to ramp up. "But that's not all there is to cryptozoology. It is called by many a pseudoscience but it is actually the amalgamation of many different branches of study. It combines biology, history, media studies, folklore and about a dozen other branches of science and humanities into one."

"So you're saying you chase monsters?!" Someone shouted out from the back.

Devon laughed and shook her head.

"No, I don't," she said. She clicked a button on the remote in her hand and the slideshow began. "I disprove monsters."

A video began to play, the sound muted, of something moving through a collection of trees. The image was shaky, zooming in and out seemingly at random and never showing the creature that moved through the trees clearly.

"Using all the advantages of modern technology I track apparent monster sightings," she began. The screen showed a reel of different headlines from local newspapers. "Using the internet, community websites, Facebook, YouTube, Instagram and all sorts of other social media I find out where people are seeing the monsters and I go there."

"Have you ever found a real one?" someone else called out.

"No," she said with a laugh, "I am pleased to say that I have never discovered a real cryptid. That's the term we 'monster hunters' use when we refer to the beasts and creatures of myth and folklore. And folklore is very important in what I do. Can anyone guess why?"

Someone hesitantly raised their hand towards the back of the room. She smiled at them and pointed. The student paused before she spoke, her face grew red as people turned to look at her.

"Is it because ancient beliefs were used to explain natural occurrences in the old days?" she asked quietly.

"Go on..." Devon encouraged. "Explain what you mean."

"Well..." the student hesitated. "Things would happen back then. But they wouldn't understand them. Lightening, thunder, death and disease, none of it was really understood. So ancient man made up myths and legends to explain them all. And the myths had creatures in them to explain the living things that they couldn't understand. Over time, as we began to understand the world better, the myths fell out of use but the stories about creatures remained behind. And now, when nothing else can explain what people see, they fall back on those stories to explain it."

"Well done young lady!" Devon said, her smile growing wide. "That is precisely it. We may have modern science and technology to explain the world to us. We might be able to know what's going on over in China or what the gross national income of Botswana is but if something strange happens, if we see a shadow in the night that we don't recognise, well....We can fall back on old patterns. We return to the stories of our childhood, of our communities. Those stories will have been handed down generation to generation and even though they may be twisted the essence may remain the same. Besides, we all love a good ghost story."

The lecture room broke out in laughter at that. Devon joined in. She clicked the button on the remote again and the image changed once more. It was a headline from a small newspaper in the south-west of England.

BEAST RETURNS AND KILLS SHEEP HERD.

There was a blurred image of a boar like creature beneath and a pencil sketch from the nineteenth Century of a tusked boar with bear like feet.

"Let's look at the Beast of Dean," Devon said. "It was my most recent case."

The image changed again with a click and a collection of dead sheep were shown on screen. There were groans of disgust.

"Come on now," Devon said with a grin. "You're going to be dealing with much worse if you're going to become vets. Now, the Beast of Dean was a monster that's first recorded sighting was in 1802. Many said that it lived in the Forest of Dean and that it looked like a large boar but monstrously disfigured. It crushed hedges, fences, it felled trees. Children went missing, probably lost in the forest, and people said that the beast had taken off with them."

She clicked the button again and the headline returned. This time the print was different, the font older, more oddly spaced. There were no photographs on the page.

"This clipping is from the local newspaper in 1802," Devon said loudly. "The local farmers, tired of having their livestock ripped to shreds and their fences crushed and broken, put together a raiding party to hunt and track the beast. Hunters from all over the country came to join in."

There was a sketch from the paper on screen now. It showed a massive group of people all filing into the forest. It was replaced with another headline.

NO SIGN OF THE BEAST.

"All of the hunters returned, none the worse from their trip," Devon said. "Except for a few blisters." People laughed and she smiled. "But there was no sighting of the beast. There were no tracks, no trails, no clue as to where the beast had gone or even if there had been a beast. People called it the Moose-Pig as well, it was so big. It stood to reason that there would have been some sort of trail left. The best trackers that could be found had travelled to the Forest, men who prided themselves on being able to track anything. None of them found a thing."

"Couldn't it have just been a big boar?" someone called out.

"That's what people might have thought," Devon said. "Except...it was a well-known fact that there were no more wild boars in the area at the time. Or anywhere else in England. They were...extinct."

She clicked the button again and a series of images of newspaper clippings began to play. They were all headlines with the dates attached. All spoke of the Beast of Dean but from different years.

"The sightings continued though, through the years," she said. "Never close together and the destruction left by the beast was never as bad as when it was first seen. Each sighting was met with more searching and every time they found nothing. That was until three months ago."

The slideshow of images stopped on the original picture that had started it all, the mass of sheep, slaughtered and the nineteenth century sketch.

"Three months ago, a farmer's herd of sheep were found killed," Devon said grimly. "They had been gutted, thrown around like they were nothing. But, and this is a big but, no parts of them were missing. They had not been eaten. Most of the injuries weren't consistent with those left by a predator. And the only tracks were those of pigs and sheep. I'd like to mention here that the farmer did have a tendency to keep his sheep and pigs in the same fields, lord knows why."

"Couldn't it have been kids?" one of the students asked. "They heard the story and decided to have some fun."

"That's what people thought as well," Devon said, her face growing grimmer. "The local police and government put a curfew in place and demanded parents keep their children in view of them at night. It led to a lot of unhappy teenagers but it also ruled them out when three nights later this happened."

She clicked the button and a new slide came up. It was of a barn. The side had been torn open, shards of wood lay everywhere. Bales of hay had been torn apart, bags of feed scattered and trampled.

"The farmer's barn was almost destroyed," she said. "The majority of his winter feeds were either consumed or damaged beyond salvation. This meant major trouble for him. If he has no feed he can't feed his animals through the winter. If he can't feed his animals he has to either slaughter them or sell them. If he has no herd come spring he can't begin lambing or breeding and preparing for sale come the summer. I think you can all appreciate how serious that would be for someone whose income relies on the steady and reliable turn of the years."

A low hum of agreement filled the room. Devon looked around and saw heads nodding. She smiled in satisfaction. Sometimes it was easy for people to forget that these weren't just monster sightings, things out of stories come to life. They were real events that had real impact on people that could last for months, even years.

"Thankfully the community was very tight knit," Devon continued. "They banded together and helped pay for the barn to be repaired and more feed to be brought in. Even the local teenagers helped out now that they were off the hook."

"Couldn't they have snuck out, broken curfew or something?" someone asked. "I mean, come on, you know what we were like when we were younger. We'd find a way to get to the party no matter what."

"Indeed," Devon said with a smile. "But the entire area around the barn was checked for any sign of human activity, excluding the farmer and his immediate family and workers. The only thing that they found in the churned up mud were a few smeared animal tracks. This was an area of high traffic remember so that wouldn't have been that unusual. All the teenagers were appalled at what had happened as well, they all went to school with the farmer's daughter and let me tell you, she was one popular young lady. Then, three more days later another farmer was hit. Or at least, almost."

She pressed a button and a video began to play. It was a night vision image of something moving around in the yard of a farm, staying close to the edges of the buildings. Then a blur moved across the yard, almost too quick to be seen. Devon pressed a button. The video rewound. She pressed again and it played once more, slower now, the frames flipping by every second. The blur moved across the yard much more slowly but it was still unclear. She pressed a button again, the video rewound a few frames and she hit pause.

There, in the middle of the farmyard was a boar. It was hideous though, nothing like a normal boar. It had wide curving tusks, thick black hair that grew in sparse patches all over its hide. There were open sores that glistened wetly in the light of the camera. Its ears were ragged and torn, almost the entire size of its head.

"Ladies and gentlemen," Devon said, a hint of pride made its way into her voice. "I give you, the Beast of Dean, in the flesh, in the modern era."

The lecture hall broke out in whispers and excited chatter.

"After this image was captured I was called in," she said, raising her voice to be heard. Silence quickly fell. "I have friends in numerous police forces, a widespread internet presence and several people who call themselves my minions who scan for things like these and let me know. A friend on the Gloucestershire constabulary passed my name on to the local authorities and after a bit of checking they called me. At the same time, one of my... minions... found these images all over social media and passed it on to me. Needless to say, within an hour of being contacted I was on my way to the Forest of Dean."

"Did you find the monster?" Someone called out again.

"Indeed I did," Devon said with a nod. "I had a good team, highly trained trackers, experts in their field. And the tracks we had were good. The police had been made aware of my practices and had ensured that no one touched the tracks and kept well clear of the area. As soon as we arrived we were able to begin tracking."

She began the slideshow again, images of the tracks and her team following them.

"It took us surprisingly less time than we expected to find the beasts." Devon said. "And yes, I did say beasts. We found them in a secluded part of the forest, well away from humans. In fact we had to use our machetes to cut through the undergrowth, that's how long it had been since people had been through. Once we reached the clearing that these creatures had made their home we found something very, very unexpected. There was not just one Beast of Dean there but in fact an entire herd. We took photographs and managed to get a blood sample from a couple of them."

She clicked the button once more and this time the screen was filled with images of a herd of the beasts that had been shown on the earlier video. There were dozens of them, scattered around the clearing, all different sizes but all equally grotesque and deformed. Sores oozed. Horns and tusks curled up and spiked into their skin. The image changed once more to show one of the creatures on its side with Devon leaning over it. She was holding a syringe and an array of medical supplies lay nearby. The creature itself was almost as big as she was.

"As you can see, the beasts are incredibly large," Devon said, waving her hand at the screen. "The results from the DNA testing and species testing later revealed a very surprising secret. These are not strange monsters from the dawn of time, nor were they hybrids between moose and pigs. In reality they were simply the common wild boars."

"But they're hideous!" someone shouted. They were met with dozens of cries of agreement from all over the room.

"Indeed they are," Devon said with a small nod of her head, a gentle smile across her face. "Sadly, that's not because they're monsters, as I'm sure many of you are hoping. The reality is that these boars had grown larger than normal and were so malformed because of one simple reason. Can anyone guess?"

"Radiation!"

"Science experiments!"

"Random genetic mutation!"

"Something they ate!"

That last one was met with laughter and even Devon joined in. She shook her head eventually though.

"All wrong I'm afraid," she said. "The simple cause of their deformity is inbreeding. All of these boars are related to each other in bizarre ways. The inbreeding goes back quite a few decades as far as we can tell from the few blood samples we took. We'd need more in order to get a fuller map but we decided to simply leave these creatures to the rangers who protect the Forest of Dean."

"How did it happen?"

"Did they kill them?"

"What did the locals say?"

"Do they taste good?"

Once more people laughed and Devon once again joined in. After a moment or two she held up her hands for silence and quickly got it.

"I would answer those questions... well apart from the last one," she said. She glanced at her watch and winced. "However we are at the end of the lecture and there is another class waiting for this hall. I guess you're all just going to have to turn up next week to find out. I promise I will tell you."

The students groaned, good naturedly and with a little laughter thrown in. She leaned on her desk and watched as they packed their things away into bags and began to file out. Once the last few, who were having conversations as they left, had begun to head out she packed up her own things. Her colleague, a member of the biology department came to the stand and they shared a nod as they switched places.

CHAPTER TWO

"Hey Devon," the teaching assistant said with a smile as Devon walked into the room and collapsed into her chair with a heavy sigh. "Tough class?"

"Hey Danny," Devon said, smiling back. She leaned back in her chair and groaned. "The class was easy. It was getting away that was the hard part."

"You've got a fan club?" Danny asked, her eyebrows almost disappearing into her hair. "It's only the first day of classes! How've you managed that one?!"

"I told them about the Beast of Dean," Devon said with a heavy sigh. "And then I didn't finish the story so they had to come back next class."

"So they waylaid you after class then?" Danny asked. "Trying to get you to tell them early. Smart. Stupid and annoying. But smart."

"The way I remember it you were one of those kids once," Devon said, glancing at Danny with a fond smile. "Didn't you keep appearing at the door to my office and badger me in to telling you more stories?"

"Yeah," Danny said, "Because I was a fan! Not because I wanted to know so I could skip the next class if I wanted to."

"True," Devon said, nodding her head in acknowledgement. "And it did pay off in the end for you. How's the reading going for Professor Malcolms anyway?"

"Horribly," Danny said, throwing herself back on to the sofa. "He's got us reading some boring 18th century tome about how to avoid being eaten by dragons or something."

"Well, just suck it -" Devon started to say.

She was interrupted by a sharp and loud knock at the door.

She and Danny shared confused glances before Danny put her book down and hurried over to open it.

"Devon Childs?" the man on the other side asked, a strong Scottish accent making it almost impossible to understand what he was saying. "I have a proposition for you."

Danny looked him up and down.

"I might take you up on it," she said with a sly smile. "I do like a Scot. However, I'm just a lowly teaching and research assistant. You need the lady by the desk."

Danny stepped aside and let the man into the office. He turned to look at her pointedly. She giggled and did a strange squatting dance.

"I'll just be going now," she said quietly. She turned and headed out the door.

Before she shut the door though she mouthed all sorts of obscene and dirty comments at Devon from behind the man's back. Devon fought hard to hide her laughter and smile.

"Professor Devon Childs?" the man asked again once the door was shut. "Monster hunter?"

"Yes, that is me," Devon said, standing to shake the man's hand before she sat back down again. "What can I do for you Mr...?"

"McCallum, Jim McCallum," he said, taking the seat opposite Devon without prompting. He leaned back in his chair and crossed one leg over the other, resting his ankle on his knee. His arms spread over the back of the seat. He looked like he owned the place. "I need your help."

"Most people do when they refer to me as a monster hunter," Devon said. The back of her neck was itching and she shifted in her seat. "So, what exactly do you need my help with?"

"I'm an entrepreneur Miss Childs," Jim said.

"Professor," Devon said quickly.

She blinked. Jim blinked. She was slightly taken aback at herself. Normally she didn't care about her title being used correctly but in this instance she felt like she needed to make it clear exactly how accomplished she was.

"Professor Childs," Jim said slowly. "I specialise in the leisure industry, particularly hotels and resorts that cater to all kinds of people, from the more relaxed to those seeking a little more... adventure."

"Ok..." Devon said. "And how do I come in to this?"

"I'm looking to build a new series of resorts on Loch Ness," Jim said. He looked at her, staring almost.

"Oh..." Devon said. Her mouth thinned until her lips were nothing more than two slim lines. "I see."

"I thought you would," Jim said with a cocky smile. "Needless to say I've been having a bit of difficulty with the locals. They're very much opposed to my building around the loch. Nessie is big business for those guys, it's one of the main reasons the local villages still exist. They think that if I build around the loch then Nessie will get scared off and no more tourists will come to see her. Him. Whatever. It's all crap of course but their disagreements are making it difficult for me to acquire the local permits."

"I see," Devon said quietly. "And you want me to prove, once and for all that there is no Loch Ness Monster, despite the fact that for decades people have been doing just that."

"Exactly," Jim said proudly. "Unfortunately the locals tend to ignore those people. They're not recognised in their fields as having the right background or knowledge."

"And what makes me any different?" Devon asked. "To be honest Mr. McCallum it sounds like a waste of time for everyone involved."

"It isn't!" Jim said, shooting to his feet and planting his hands on the desk. "You're a well-known monster hunter. You have a history of proving time and again that monsters don't exist. You are a recognised and respected expert in the field of make believe monsters and proving they're not real."

"Cryptozoology," Devon said coldly. "And I never set out to prove that cryptids don't exist. I set out to see if they're real and find out the truth."

"Miss Childs... Professor Childs," Jim said. "We both know that there's no such thing as the Loch Ness Monster. Everyone knows it but these guys up at the loch won't let it go. If you can provide documented evidence that Nessie isn't real then I can get my permits."

"It's been done Mr. McCallum," Devon said with a sigh. "I'd be going over ground that's been trampled over a thousand times before. There's nothing new in it for me, no mystery, no excitement. I enjoy the thrill of the chase and the chance, even for a few days, that the cryptids I'm looking for might be real. There is nothing like that for me there. I'm sorry but you'll need to find someone else. I can give you some names but I won't be coming."

"Will £500,000 change your mind?" Jim said suddenly. "It'll be easy work after all, everyone's already done the work for you. You come, you poke around, do whatever it is you do and then say there's no Nessie."

Devon kept her eyes locked on the desk. Her heart was racing. That amount of money was more than she could ever have hoped for. She could fund her research for a very long time with it. She could travel and go to the places that she'd never been to before but always wanted to go to. She could search for cryptids that were international legends. She could set up digs in dozens of countries. She glanced up at Jim. He had a cocky smirk on his face and she wanted to knock it off but the money. Oh god the money.

"I do things my way," she said firmly. "If I'm going to do this I do it the way I always do. You have to understand that I'm not setting out to disprove Nessie's existence. I'm doing it to see if she's there or what other reasons there might be for the stories. Do you understand?"

"Of course," Jim said with a firm nod. "When can you leave?"

"In a few hours," Devon said, climbing to her feet. "I'll pack my bags, sort out some time off with the dean and get Danny to arrange my flight up there. If I feel I need them once I'm there, my team will join me in a few days."

"Don't worry about the flight," Jim said firmly. "I have a helicopter at the local airport. We can head up there together."

"Oh. Ok," Devon said quickly. "I'll meet you at the airport in a couple of hours."

"Wonderful." Jim said. He reached out and shook Devon's hand. "It's wonderful doing business with you."

He turned and let himself out of the office. Devon watched him go and collapsed on to her chair. She gave a disbelieving laugh at what had just happened. Danny slowly edged in through the open door.

"You ok boss lady?" she asked quietly. "You kind of look like you've been told something either really scary or really amazing."

"I think it's both," Devon said. Her voice was breathy and airy. "Oh my god. What did I just do?"

"What did you do?" Danny asked. "Who did you do? Oh my god! Did you do the Scottish Hottie?!"

Devon blinked and returned to herself. She stared at Danny.

"The Scottish Hottie?!" Devon asked. "Where do you come up with this stuff?"

"What?" Danny said with a shrug. "He's hot and he's Scottish. I thought it was obvious." She threw herself into the chair that Jim had previously been sitting in, her legs dangling over one arm. "So, if you two didn't bang what did he want?"

"He wants me to go to Loch Ness and disprove the existence of Nessie so that he can build a bunch of hotels there," Devon said.

"So if you turned him down why did he look so happy?" Danny asked.

"I took him up on his offer," Devon said reluctantly.

"What?!" Danny shrieked. "But it's Loch Ness. It's been done. There's nothing there that's exciting or new. At least the Forest of Dean had hot police men and a real mystery!"

"He offered me a lot of money," Devon said with a sigh. "And I mean A LOT. We could both pay off our student loans with it and still have loads left over."

"How much is a lot?" Danny said slowly. Her head was cocked to one side lending her the air of a confused spaniel.

"500 grand," Devon said.

"Oh. My. God!" Danny cried. She shrieked and leapt to her feet. "Oh my god. Oh my god. Oh my god. When do you leave?"

"In a few hours," Devon said. "I'm meeting him at the airport and we're flying up in his helicopter."

Danny let out a low whistle, her eyebrows once more almost disappearing into her hair.

"Impressive," she said eventually.

"I know," Devon said. She paused and shook her head. "There's something about this though. And him. Something's not quite right with it all. Can you do me a favour while I go and pack?"

"Sure," Danny said. "As long as it's not too much hard work or too boring."

"You'll like it, I promise," Devon said. She got to her feet and began to pull her things together. "I need you to find out everything you can about this guy. Jim McCallum. And I mean everything. What businesses he owns, where he came from, where he went to school. Scandals about his buildings. Anything you can think of."

"Got it," Danny said. She squeezed around Devon and took her seat. "Dig up all the dirt I can about the Scottish Hottie. Want it in a discrete folder for when you get a moment alone?"

"That would be best." Devon said. "I'll take my laptop but paper copy would be good too. If there's been objections to his buildings before, I want to know about it. I'll be back in a few hours to talk to the Department Head and the Dean about taking some time off. I'll get the folder then."

"Want me to send one of your minions to the library?" Danny asked. "Get background info about Nessie?"

"This is why you're my assistant," Devon said fondly. She leaned over and kissed Danny on the head then turned and headed to the door. "Thinking ahead and knowing what I need."

"That and I just want to make your minions suffer," Danny said with an evil grin. She waved her hands in front of herself like a puppet master. "Dance little students, dance!"

"Don't kill my minions while I'm gone," Devon said, pausing at the door. "I've just got them trained up right."

"I promise nothing!" Danny called out.

Devon shut the office door with a laugh and then hurried down the corridor.

Three hours later Devon arrived at the airport. She had two heavy bags that contained her clothes and another bag that held her laptop and all of the other equipment she needed to begin her search. The taxi driver very reluctantly helped her to load the bags on to a trolley she brought running over to them. As soon as she'd handed over the money he climbed back into the car and hightailed it out of the car park and on to the motorway. Devon was left standing on the pavement outside of departures and wondering where to go. McCallum hadn't left her any directions after that point.

"Devon!" A female voice called out. "Devon! Wait up!"

Devon looked around and saw nothing. Then a few cries came from further away and she looked over in their direction. People were shoved to one side, luggage knocked over. The person responsible was a young woman. Devon groaned. It was Danny.

"Thank god I found you," Danny said when she reached Devon. She leaned her hands on her knees and gasped for breath. "I thought I was gonna miss you."

"Me too," Devon said as she looked down at her friend. "What did you find?"

"A lot," Danny said as she stood up straight. "I got half of your minions looking up about McCallum. It's all in the files, both paper and hard drive. And then as soon as I told your minions where you were going, they got together and started to look up what they could find about Nessie."

"I'm guessing that they found a lot," Devon said.

"Yup," Danny said.

She straightened and held out the rucksack. Devon took it and opened it. Inside were manila folders and packs of paper. There was a hint of shining black at the bottom of the compartment and a matte black rectangle. Something hard pressed against her hand in one of the pockets. She shifted her grip and opened the pocket to see a few flash drives.

"You've got the info about McCallum in there," Danny said. "It's in the blue folders. The red ones have the cliff notes version of all the Nessie information we could find; history, images, first hand reports. The flash drives have more information on it and so does the hard drive in the bottom of the bag. We filled up an eReader with all the books we could find about Nessie. There's a lot of reading there."

"You are a star," Devon said, hugging Danny tightly. "I think this should be everything I need. I'll make sure I get in touch if there's anything else."

"No problem boss lady," Danny said with a wide grin. "Just remember, if you need me up there I'll be there straight away. And if you don't, try to bring me back a hunky Scot."

"I'll do my best," Devon said with a laugh. "They might not like me much though, I am trying to disprove their local legend after all."

"Oh come on," Danny said, rubbing Devon's arm. "You're not trying to disprove Nessie's existence, you're just trying to find out if she's real or not."

"Either way, I'm going to face trouble and we both know it," Devon said. She gave a heavy sigh. "Well, I better get going and find McCallum."

"No need," Danny said, nodding towards a spot behind Devon's right shoulder. "Here he comes now,"

Devon turned and saw McCallum striding through the crowd. They parted before him without a thought, it was like he oozed an aura that told them they should move. He strode over to Devon and smiled broadly. Then he gave her a hug.

"Dr. Childs," he said as he stepped back. "So glad you could make it."

Devon smiled and nodded.

"Well, come along, my helicopter is waiting for us," he said confidently. "No need to wait."

"I'll see you later Devon," Danny said, turning away. "Let me know when you get there."

She disappeared into the crowd, Devon watched her go. She turned back to McCallum and found him looking her up and down. He smiled again when she caught his eye.

"Well, let's get going," he said.

He took hold of her trolley and headed off towards the Departures bay. She put the rucksack Danny had given her over her shoulder, picked up her other bag and followed behind meekly.

***

The flight was uneventful. Devon spent most of it reading about Nessie on the eReader Danny had passed on to her. McCallum had tried to entice her into conversation but she hadn't been able to hear him properly and it had dwindled into silence. A tap on her thigh after an hour or so brought her attention back to her surroundings.

"We're approaching Loch Ness now," McCallum shouted, trying his best to be heard over the roar of the engines. "Thought you might want to get a good look."

Devon lowered her eReader to her knee and looked out of the window. She gasped as she saw the infamous loch for the first time. It stretched for miles between two rows of mountains. The waters were deep and dark, green and swirling. Roads ran along the edges, small houses and people moved down below, looking like ants. Crowds gathered at the loch's shore, tour buses waited nearby. The helicopter circled the loch, travelling rapidly around its awkward circumference and giving Devon a good view of it all. It was breathtaking.

Then they started to descend, close to a small town near the loch. A crowd gathered in the square to watch and they quickly fell out of sight as the helicopter disappeared behind a strand of trees to land in a car park that was suspiciously empty of cars. Devon put the eReader back in its bag and waited for the engines to cease their roar.

"I've made you a booking at a local Bed and Breakfast," McCallum said, his voice a little lower now. "It's not the best there is but the food's pretty decent and there are a few good reviews for it. I can't guarantee a warm welcome though."

"There never is one," Devon said, gathering her things together. "You get used to it."

She climbed out of the helicopter, keeping her head low. A man hurried forwards to help her unload her bags and he put them into a shopping trolley of all things. She smirked at that but followed him as he led her to the road. At the entrance to the car park she heard the helicopter engines fire up again and the wind around them picked up. She turned and watched as the copter rose in to the sky, taking her new employer with it.

"He never sticks around long," the man beside her said. "Comes in, drops off whichever bunch of experts he's brought along and then gets going. The locals don't like him much and I can't say I blame them."

"Are you a local?" Devon asked as she followed her new guide along the road. "Have you seen Nessie?"

"I'm as local as they come," the guy said proudly. "Can't say I've ever seen the monster but I think it's real enough. And I reckon you'll soon find out yourself."

"I get the feeling it won't be easy," Devon said.

"Oh no, it won't," the man said with a laugh. "But nothing fun ever is."

Devon laughed and kept following him. He led her to a small building decorated with ivy and flowers in hanging baskets. There was a small, neat sign over the entrance, declaring it a B & B. The man unloaded her bags and headed away.

"The booking's under your name," he called over his shoulder as he wheeled his cart away. "Good luck!"

She called her goodbyes after him and started to haul her bags up the steps. A man rushed out and grabbed them from her, carrying them inside. She stepped back, slightly startled and watched as he did it. Then he turned to face her and smiled.

"Welcome to Loch Ness," he said with a thick Scottish accent. "Glad you decided to stay with us. What's the name?"

"Childs," Devon said, following him in. "Doctor Devon Childs."

He froze for a moment when she said her name and then continued walking. His entire demeanour had changed by the time they reached the reception desk, a little table nestled beneath the stairs. He was tense, wound tight and when he turned to look at her again his smile was gone.

"You're in room 33 on the second floor," he said handing over her key. "Breakfast is 6:30 till 9, you'll have to find your own lunch and dinner but we serve both in the bar through that door."

He disappeared through said door, leaving Devon alone in the entrance hall with her bags and the stairs.

"Well that didn't take long," she said with a heavy sigh. "Guess I'm carrying these for myself now."

She grabbed her bags, hefting them and shifting her grip until they were balanced well enough for her to tackle the stairs. She started up. She could already hear the conversations going on in the bar, the anger in the voices. She gave a sigh as she walked and eventually the voices faded away. It was going to be a long week.

***

Just as she'd expected, the reception when she entered the bar was frosty at best. She'd not bothered to unpack her things in her room, lovely though it was. Her stomach had been growling since she'd flown over Newcastle and it had only gotten louder since then. She needed food and figured that the bar was the best place to get it. When she stepped in though all conversation faded away and everyone turned to stare at her. Her step faltered for a minute but she took a deep breath and carried on towards the bar itself.

"Pint of lemonade please," she said with a smile at that same man who had checked her in. "And can I see a menu?"

"Sure," he said curtly, tossing a menu on to the bar and turning to get her drink order.

She looked through the menu, her stomach growling louder and louder with each item that she read. There was so much choice and she couldn't decide.

"So…" a voice said behind her. She turned to see that it belonged to a burly man, well into middle age who was swaying as he stood there holding his pint. "This is the city girl come all the way out here to prove us locals are all idiots."

"Lay off Jack," the bartender said as he poured Devon's drink. "I've warned you already about this."

"It's ok," Devon said in a quiet voice, "I expected this."

"Yeah Jamie," Jack said loudly. "She knows she's not welcome here. She's just too stubborn to know it I reckon. Big city girl like her, probably thinks she's got the right to stay where she isn't wanted and poke her nose in to things that aren't her business."

"I was hired to do a job," Devon said slowly, the speech well rehearsed. "I'm not trying to poke my nose in or any of the other things you think I'm here for."

"Bollocks!" a man shouted out from another table. "You're on McCallum's payroll, just like all the rest. You'll do what he tells you and fuck us all over with your fancy science."

"Yeah," Jack said harshly. "You'll turn around at the end of the week and tell us all the Nessie doesn't exist, just like McCallum is paying you to say. You've done it all over the place and we know it. Now you're going to do it to us and leave us screwed."

"Mr. Jack," Devon said, standing up tall. Anger made her bristle and her stomach burned. "I am simply here to prove whether the Loch Ness Monster is real or not. I am not here to do as McCallum orders me to, I won't say that Nessie isn't real unless I find that she isn't. I know how important the legend is to you around here and I wouldn't want to damage that without proof."

"You don't give a shit about us," the man from the table shouted out. "You just get your kicks proving things don't exist and leaving the people who rely on the money from that business high and dry with no more income."

"I am well aware of how important Nessie tourism is to you all here," Devon said harshly. "I will not damage that if I can help it. I am solely interested in the creature, first finding out whether she is real and then what she is. Let me assure you that nothing would make me happier than discovering that Nessie is very much real and very much alive in your loch."

"Yeah right," Jack said. He turned around and headed back to his table. "You'll say she's not, mark my words. McCallum wants you to say that so you will, just like all the other 'experts' he's brought in."

Devon opened her mouth but closed it again. There was no point trying to argue with these men. They'd made their minds up about her and about what she was going to do. It wasn't unusual. She'd gone to dozens of places that relied on the income from local legends and received exactly the same sort of welcome. Loch Ness was no exception. She'd learnt the hard way that trying to argue with the locals was pointless until she had evidence to back herself up. She had none of that right now. But she did wish that they hadn't made their minds up simply because of who she was working for. McCallum had really angered these people and she had made them just as angry by being connected to him.

The thud of her lemonade being placed on the bar made her turn and she finally decided on what her lunch would be.

CHAPTER THREE

Devon spent the next few days doing what she did best; searching for proof that the legend she was seeking was real. She spoke to the local boatmen, anyone who had a boat and would be willing to take her out. Many had tales of having seen the creature but none were willing to take her out on to the loch, even to scan with sonar. Eventually she found one who believed that she only wanted to find out the truth, that she wasn't just pretending to look before agreeing with McCallum. He had a story of his own about seeing the monster, many people told her that he actually claimed to have interacted with it but no matter how much she asked he would never tell her the story.

What he did do however was allow her to attach her sonar rig to the bottom of the boat and track in long swathes across the top of the loch. He even provided her with the most accurate and up to date map that he could of the loch. They spent their days going back and forth across the lake's surface; the boatman, Arthur's eyes fixed on the surface of the loch and Devon's locked on to the sonar read out screen. Each little blip on the screen made her heart leap in to her throat and she'd call for another, closer look on that particular location. Arthur would mark the sighting on the map they had and then steer the boat to circle around until the reading became clearer.

Sometimes they would have to weigh anchor and allow Devon to let out her remote operated aquatic camera to go in for a closer look and to get a clearer view of the murky depths. Usually it was just fish though, swimming and darting around as they played in the shallows. Once or twice there were otters on the screen, chasing the fish for their dinner. Sometimes, however, there would be something else, a large shadow that lay just out of reach of the camera's lights. It would flicker in the deep green depths, flashing in and out of sight but never getting close enough for a clear look. Devon would attempt to chase the shadow but it would disappear and Arthur would mark the sighting on the map once more.

Devon spent her nights in her room, poring over maps and photographs, trawling through the dozens of videos that her students had piled on to the hard drive. Her head spun with all of the theories that she read in the books, the images that she had seen and all of the arguments that had been made for and against the existence of Nessie. She'd fall asleep, exhausted and fully clothed on the top of her bed, waking the next morning with aches and pains and a fuzzy brain.

As the days passed and she got no closer to proving the monster's existence, she began to lose her energy. The thrill of the search, the excitement of each potential sighting was fading away, becoming only a mere flicker. Each time she saw a video or a photograph that looked like it could be real someone else would debunk it, prove that it was a fake. She felt like she was retreading the same ground that dozens of people before her had taken, nothing new was coming in. It was why she had been so reluctant to take on the job in the first place. She had known that there would be nothing new.

The occasional chat with Danny in the evenings was what kept her going really. The other woman's energy and belief in what Devon did and the possibility, however small, of Nessie's existence filled Devon with just enough hope to make her get out of bed the morning after and helped to drive her to keep looking. One night though, that all changed.

CHAPTER FOUR

She was sleeping, still dressed and face down on an open book when the shouting started. She woke up, startled and disorientated, not quite knowing where she was. The shouting kept going though and a look around the room reminded her of where she was and what she was here to do. She considered just getting into her night clothes and climbing into bed properly, planning on ignoring the shouting downstairs when four words caught her attention.

"It was the monster!" a woman's voice all but screamed.

Devon was on her feet in an instant and racing down the stairs before she could think. At the bottom of the stairs she was met by a crowd of people, worried and scared looks on their faces. They were crowded together, holding each other and all talking loudly, at the same time, over the top of each other. Some of them turned to look at her and sent glares in her direction.

"It's her fault!" screamed the same woman before as she pointed at Devon. "It's all her fault."

"What's my fault?" Devon asked quietly as she stepped down on to the main floor. "What's going on?"

"Someone's been killed," said Jamie, the hotel owner. "Down by the loch. They're saying the monster got him. He's been torn to pieces."

"What?!" Devon gasped. "How? What was he even doing out there at night?"

"Does it matter?" growled Jack as he stamped towards her. "He's dead because of you."

"What? Why me?" Devon asked. "I've been asleep in my room."

"You've made the monster angry!" Jack cried out. "We all see you, day after day, going up and down the loch in that boat. Chasing after the poor thing. It's upset and it's taking it out on us. She killed that man as a warning. You need to go."

"That is ridiculous," Devon snapped. "If there is a monster it won't think like us and it certainly wouldn't just kill to send a warning. No animal in nature does that. They kill to eat and to protect themselves. We're the only ones who kill for other reasons."

"It's your fault and you know it!" Jack shouted. He towered over Devon, glaring down at her.

"That's enough Jack!" a new voice snapped.

Everyone fell silent and turned to look at the newcomer who stood in the doorway. Jack stepped away from Devon but continued to glare at her. The man in the doorway stepped forwards, out of the shadows. It was a man wearing the uniform of a police officer.

"Dr. Childs?" he asked, walking towards her. She nodded. "I'm Chief McIntyre, head of the local constabulary. I trust you've heard about the death tonight?" She nodded again. "Good. Well....We need your help."

This was met by shouts of anger and confusion from the assembled crowd. They demanded to know why Devon was being called in to help, why they would use her when she'd already upset the monster of the loch.

"Because I say so!" the police chief shouted. "Now go back to your homes. Dr. Childs, please come with me."

Devon nodded and followed the chief outside. They walked down the street side by side.

"I'm not happy about this," the chief muttered quietly. "We've not had an unexplained death here in decades, let alone anything like this. We're just not equipped for it, we don't have the man power or the skill set."

"So why come to me?" Devon asked, "I'm not a pathologist."

"No you're not," the chief said. "You're a crypto-zoologist. But you're also an expert in animals and the marks that they leave. That's why we need you."

"To look at the body?" Devon asked. "So you can find the animal responsible?"

"Exactly," the chief said. He stopped and stared at the sky. "For all intents and purposes it looks like this man was killed by the monster, or at least an animal with claws and teeth and that was strong enough to do this."

"But you're not sure..." Devon filled in.

"No," he said, looking right at her. "Something about this isn't sitting right with me. The pathologist, our local doctor, he can give the true cause of death but we can't read the markings left by whatever killed the man. I need you to look at the body and examine those markings. I'll provide whatever you need. But I need to know if it was an animal and if it was, what animal. If there's a creature out there that's killing people, my people, I need to know and I need to know how to catch it so I can keep my people safe."

"I understand," Devon said with a nod. They started walking again. "Truth be told this is where I normally get called in. Mysterious deaths, strange injuries, animal bodies turning up. That's when people normally call me for my help. I don't enjoy proving local legends wrong, believe me."

"Oh I do," the chief said. "I made a point of studying your history and getting in touch with a few of the other chiefs that you've helped out. The way I see it is you're a police officer for the animal kingdom."

"That's a new one," Devon said.

They stopped outside a small stone building. There were a few pale faced police officers sitting on the wall nearby. One was leaning over and she could hear the sound of retching. The chief turned to her.

"This isn't going to be pretty I'm afraid," he said. "Are you sure you can handle it? I can get pictures taken and sent to you if you'd prefer?"

"No," Devon said firmly. "I've got a strong stomach. You can't operate on an animal's insides if you don't. Besides, I prefer to see the injuries for myself if you don't mind."

"Not at all," the chief said. "Right this way."

He led her into the building and down a long corridor. He stopped outside of an iron door and handed her gloves, a hair net and a long white coat before putting his own on.

"This is usually our funeral parlour," he said, his voice muffled. "It serves the entire area for about 50 miles all around. It's never busy but it's got a steady stream of customers."

"Death waits for no man," Devon said. "Shall we go in then?"

The chief nodded and opened the door. Devon went in and was immediately hit by a wave of cold and then the smell of death and embalming chemicals. In the centre of the room was a metal table with a blood covered corpse laying on it. Massive chunks of flesh were missing, revealing the red muscle and yellow fat beneath. White ones glinted in the bright light that hung over the body. Another man in a white coat leaned over the body, examining it and he barely looked up as they entered. Devon nodded her hello when he looked at her though and went straight to the body. The chief hovered behind her, closer to the wall than to the body.

She leaned over the body, looking at the wounds that she

could see.

"They were definitely made by something sharp," she said, talking aloud to herself. "And curved, definitely. There's just something..."

She leaned in closer, her hands gently reaching out to push and pull at the cold flesh. Silence filled the room as she looked, examining each and every wound that she could see. The pathologist on the other side of the table would point something out now and then and helped her to move the body when she asked. It was a long process and soon extra light was coming into the room from the windows high up on the walls. Dawn was breaking.

She eventually straightened, groaning at the pain in her back. She washed off and followed the pathologist and the police chief out of the room.

"Well?" the chief asked.

"He died of blood loss," the pathologist said. "Those injuries were deep and he would have lost a lot of blood within minutes. Alone that would have been enough. But a few of the cuts were over major arteries and veins. It would have taken seconds. Probably not even long enough for him to feel much pain. The marks were definitely made with something sharp, very sharp."

"So he probably didn't suffer then," the chief said. He sighed heavily. "That's something at least."

"A lot of the wounds seemed to have been inflicted after death occurred," the pathologist continued. "There weren't the same bruising or blood within the wounds like with the others. They were all consistent with the same source but not all done at the same time. The worst of the wounds, particularly the parts where flesh was removed almost down to the bone... that was all done post mortem."

"Dr. Childs?" the chief asked, looking at Devon.

"Those wounds are definitely strange," she said. "I've never seen anything quite like them before. They look at a glance like they could have come from an animal, the damage is consistent with animal attacks that I've examined before."

"So what animal was it?" Chief McIntyre asked quickly. "Do I need to clear the area?"

"I don't think it was an animal," Devon said with a shrug. "I've seen the results of animal attacks, many, many times. They look like they could have been done by an animal sure, or at least that's what it's supposed to look like. But an animal did not do that."

"How can you be sure?" the chief asked quickly. "Are you completely sure?"

"I'd stake my reputation on it," Devon said. "Whoever did this wanted you to think that it was an animal but it wasn't. Those injuries, all of the markings, they're too precise and surgical. There's no imperfections in them like there would be with an animal's claws or teeth. Whatever made those wounds had no damage done to it. Any animal capable of causing that sort of damage would have already gained damage to themselves."

"Anything else?" the chief said as he made notes in his notebook. "Besides the injuries themselves?"

"That isn't enough?" Devon asked. The chief shook his head. She sighed. "Fine, aside from this gut feeling I have... it's the way the attack looks to have gone down. Like the doctor said, the worst of the injuries came after death. That's not how animals attacking humans work, not at all. They do the worst damage when you're alive and if they attack for protection... once you're dead and stop moving they lose interest and wander off."

"Couldn't it have been eating this guy?" the chief asked. "I mean, that'd account for the missing chunks of flesh."

"Normally I'd say yes," Devon admitted, "But the wounds aren't right for an animal, no animal that I know of, making a meal out of our friend in there. There's not enough tearing to the flesh around the wounds. If I'm completely honest it looks like the flesh has been hacked away with a blade or something, not torn off like a predator would do."

"Are you saying that a person did this?" the chief asked after a moment's pause. "That... someone, here in town, killed this man?"

"I think so," Devon said sadly. "The markings are too regular and precise to be an animal. None of them cross over each other. Animals claw and bite and scratch in any pattern that they want. They go after limbs and the throat. They have no specific aim but it looks to me like a lot of the damage was done to hit the major arteries. I'm afraid that you're probably looking at a human culprit."

"Probably?" the chief asked. "I thought you were staking your reputation on this?"

"I am," Devon said, "But I'm still human. I could be wrong but I don't think I am."

The chief hung his head and gave a heavy sigh.

"Ok then," he said. "I guess we need to go and tell everyone."

"Now?" Devon asked in surprise. "Won't they be in bed?"

"Dr. Childs, you really don't know small towns do you?" the chief said, as though he were talking to a child. "The news will have spread by now and everyone in the village will be waiting outside for us to come out."

"Oh..." Devon said. "Right..."

"I can go and tell them myself if you want?" the chief said, a little more kindly. "You can go back to your room and get some sleep."

"No, it's ok," Devon said, pulling off her protective equipment. "I doubt I'll be able to get much sleep now anyway. It's one thing when an animal does this, they're just following instinct. But a human..." she shuddered. "That's deliberate and knowing someone can do that to another person..."

"I know what you mean," the chief said, joining her in removing his gear. "Let's go and face them then."

Just as the Chief of police had predicted they were met with a mob of people when they exited the funeral parlour. They were all shouting out questions, barely held back by the few officers that formed a line between them and Devon, the Chief and the doctor. A box had been brought over, long and wide enough for all three of them to stand on, side by side. The Chief climbed up and helped Devon up beside him.

"Alright everybody," he called out. "Settle down, settle down!"

"We don't wanna settle down!" someone shouted. "We want answers!"

"Someone's been killed by the monster!" another person shouted. "What the hell is that woman still doing here? She's the one who pissed it off!"

"That's enough!" the Chief shouted. "I asked Dr. Childs to assist in our investigation due to her expertise. That is why she's here. Anyone who has a problem with that can take it up with me."

He stared at the crowd for a long time, not saying a word, just staring. They slowly settled down and fell quiet.

"Good," he said firmly. "Now, according to the good doctor here the man was murdered and died because of his injuries. But according to both the doctor and Dr. Childs here these injuries were not inflicted by an animal of any sort. They were made by another person. And I am inclined to agree with that assessment."

"Bullshit!" someone shouted. "It was Nessie and you know it."

"It needs to be caught before anyone else dies!" another shouted out.

"Our children play in that loch, do you want them to be killed too?" someone else called. "Do something!"

"Very well, very well," the Chief said, holding up his hands to quieten them. "I ask you to keep your children out of the loch for the time being. I am sure that it wasn't the monster of the loch but whoever did this likely tossed the murder weapon into the water. Starting tomorrow I'm going to have a specialist diving team up here to search the water and look for anything that may help us to bring this man's killer to justice. I want to speak to anyone who might have seen or heard anything to do with this murder."

The crowd grumbled but said no more. The news of a potential murderer amongst them seemed to have sombered them up and calmed their anger at Devon. The chief turned to her.

"I'm assuming that you'll want to oversee our dives?" he said knowingly to her.

"You assume correctly," Devon said. "I'll watch from a distance if that's ok, but I will be on the loch's surface. I have to continue my search after all."

"Ok," the chief said, a little reluctantly. "But if you find anything..."

"I know," Devon said with a smile. "I'll call you and your men over straight away."

"Good," the chief said. "Now, you better go and get at least some sleep before tomorrow. I think it's going to be a long one."

Devon nodded, agreeing with him. She climbed down from their makeshift podium and made her way back to the B&B. She tried to ignore the stares and glares at her back and the mutterings that followed her.

CHAPTER FIVE

The next day was cold with a brisk, sharp wind that came in from the sea. Devon was glad that she'd brought her thick winter clothing as she stood shivering on the deck of Arthur's boat. The divers had begun to prepare for their work and she was watching as they piled equipment into the police boat. Arthur hadn't said a word to her when she arrived, simply nodded and helped load on some of her equipment when she'd asked. He was pale though and the dark bags under his eyes suggested that he hadn't slept much at all the night before. It wasn't a surprise though, everyone in the village looked like that.

Devon's phone rang then and she turned away from the other boat and rooted through her many pockets to find them. She stared at the name on the screen and gave a heavy sigh.

"Mr. McCallum," she said when she answered. "What can I do for you?"

"Please, call me Jack," McCallum repeated. "And I heard about what happened last night, the death of that poor man."

"You mean murder Mr. McCallum," Devon said, ignoring the man's invitation for familiarity. She didn't want to be any closer to this man than she had to be. "He was murdered McCallum, by another person."

"That's not what the papers are saying," McCallum said. "They're saying he was ripped apart by Nessie, the media's abuzz with the news."

"I saw the body myself sir," Devon said firmly. "The poor man was not killed by any animal alive or dead that's ever existed."

"That's terrible," McCallum said. He didn't sound upset though. "Of course everyone's talking about Loch Ness now.

There's so much attention being sent its way. People want to know what happened, I've already got room requests coming in at the resort!"

"Well hopefully we can get it wrapped up before too long," Devon said tonelessly. "Having a murderer on the loose might put people off."

"Of course, of course," McCallum said quickly. "Good luck and god's speed and all that."

He hung up. Devon stared at the phone in her hand and shook her head.

"The man's insane," she muttered. Then she called out to the boatman, "Arthur! How're things looking?"

"They're good lassie," Arthur said. "Everything's all set and we just need to get moving to get the readings."

Devon smiled and nodded. She turned back to the police boat. It looked like the divers were getting ready to go in. They were lined up, sitting on the side of the boat and paying attention to a stern looking man who was pacing back and forth in front of them, talking. Devon couldn't catch what was being said. Arthur started the engine and began to head towards the other boat. Devon checked on her equipment, that the monitors were working and the sonar was pinging back to them like it was supposed to. Everything seemed to be ok. Arthur poked his head out of the small shed over the helm and called out to her, trying to be heard over the sounds of the engine.

"The chief's asked us to help with the search," he shouted. "He says your sonar's far better than anything that they have on board and they want an extra set of eyes down there. The water's too dark to see clearly without it."

"Ok," Devon shouted back. "Keep pace with the police boat and stay parallel to them if you can."

Arthur nodded and ducked back into the shed. The boat shifted and started to slow. It drew up alongside the other boat and stopped there, bobbing in the water. The stern man in the other boat nodded at Devon and she waved back. She watched as one by one the divers dropped over the side and into the brackish water. Almost instantly their silhouettes pinged up on the sonar screen and she shifted the ring with her controls until the shapes were in the centre of the screen. Then she waved over at the stern man who nodded again.

The divers headed deeper and deeper into the dark water. It was cold, chilling to the bone and there was silt and sediment floating everywhere. They could barely see a thing. It didn't take long though for them to reach the bottom of the loch, where the light could barely reach. Their underwater hand torches did the trick though and they could quickly see that there was so much silt in the water that the extra light wouldn't do much good. Still they arranged themselves in a line and began to slowly swim along the bottom of the loch. Their fins churned up the muddy silt of the loch floor and visibility dropped to near zero levels. The only thing that many of them could see was swirling mud and beams of light trying to cut through it all. One cried out, the sound muffled through his mask, when something brushed against him.

Above, on the surface, Devon stared at the screen and gave a soft cry. The sonar screen was covered in large shapes that changed position constantly. They completely surrounded the divers down below.

"Sir!" she called out to the man on the police boat. "Sir, there's something on the sonar. There's a lot of them all around the divers. They're large and fast moving. They seem to be cir-cling."

"Thanks for the heads up," the man called back. "They've not seen anything yet so they're staying down."

"Sir," Devon shouted out. "With all due respect, it is my professional opinion that those men get out of there! That is the behaviour of predators preparing to attack!"

"Nonsense!" the man shouted. "There's nothing dangerous in these waters. The men can handle themselves."

"Arsehole," Devon muttered, turning back to the screen.

She bit the nail of her thumb as she watched the monitor. The shapes were definitely circling, drawing in closer and closer to the divers. She felt Arthur coming up beside her to watch the screen too.

"You really think they'll attack?" he asked her quietly.

"Yes," she said firmly. "I've seen this before, in sharks and killer whales."

"You told the captain over there?" Arthur asked.

"Of course I did," she muttered. "He's just ignoring the fact. He's going to get those men killed."

"They know what they're doing lass," Arthur said. "I know some of these men. If there's trouble they'll get out of there."

"What's that?!" Devon said. She leaned in for a closer look. "There!"

She pointed at the monitor. There was a massive shape on the screen, bigger than all of the others. It was moving quickly, heading straight for the divers and the two boats.

"Oh my god," she cried out, stepping back. "Captain! Captain, something's coming!"

She raced to the edge of the boat, trying to be heard by the men in the other craft. They weren't paying attention to her. Something bumped against the bottom of her boat, making a tremendous crashing noise and sending them rocking. She clung on to the railing and kept calling out. The other boat was set rocking, she could hear the thud of a collision. The men on the boat rushed around, back and forth. They scanned the water.

Gradually both boats stopped rocking and everything seemed to have gone still again.

"Dr. Childs," Arthur said. "It's still here."

Devon glanced at the monitor, still clutching the railing. She only got a brief glimpse of a large shape between their boats before suddenly the water in the gap between them erupted into the air. She was thrown away from the railing, back on to the deck and on her back. She heard a grunt from Arthur who had been thrown against the far railing. The boat kept rocking, hard. She could hear shouts from the other boat, cries of fear and alarm. All she could do though was hold on tight as she slammed against the railings. She kept her grip, one arm wrapped around a post. The boat rocked from side to side and she kept her eyes fixed on the water. It was frothing with white foam, churning like something was thrashing around beneath the surface.

Gradually the boat's rocking slowed and she tentatively let go. She could hear Arthur swearing behind her as she climbed to her feet and the shouts and calls from the other boat. Her eyes were fixed on the water. Dark shapes were beginning to erupt along the surface. It was the divers. They began to scramble to get out of the water, grabbing on to the ladder that led to the deck of the other boat.

"There's something down there!" one of them shouted. "It brushed right past me, sent me spinning."

"Did you see the size of that thing?!" another cried. "I didn't get a good look at it but I bet it was bigger than a double decker bus!"

"And the other things!" a third diver cried. "They were everywhere. They were massive."

"They were fast!" the first interrupted. "Sorry sir but there's no way I'm going back in there, no matter how much you pay me."

"You can't see a thing in there," the second one said as they all pulled off their gear. "The whole thing's pointless."

Devon started to tune them out. They were terrified, she could hear it in their voices. She wondered why they'd even sent in a dive team. Everyone knew that visibility in the loch was close to zero, sending in divers had just been a waste of time and money. She looked down at the water between the boats again. It had started to calm and settle down, turning back into a black plain only disturbed by a few ripples. Then a few air bubbles began to pop up, just one or two at first but they came faster and faster. The water churned once more. The boats stayed steady though. Devon held on anyway, clutching the railings so tightly that her knuckles turned white. Her eyes were fixed on the water.

Then a dark shape emerged. It burst through the surface and almost flew into the air before it settled there, floating. Devon frowned and cocked her head to the side. It looked like a person. The noise from the other boat stopped. She glanced up to see the divers and crew gathered at the edge, staring at the shape. One of them got a boat hook and hooked it. With a bit of twisting and turning they were able to turn it over. It was a body. It was a body just like the last one.

CHAPTER SIX

"I am Jacqueline Rogers, reporting for Highland News," the news reporter said as she stared at the camera, microphone held beneath her mouth. "Today a second body was pulled out of Loch Ness by police divers. They were in the water searching for evidence involved in another death discovered late last night. Police are treating it as suspicious and looking for anyone with any information to come forward. Locals however are convinced that this is the work of the infamous Loch Ness Monster, angered by current building works on the other side of the loch. Here's some footage that we managed to acquire, showing the dive team's attempts and panicked abortion of the dive."

The news reader relaxed as the controller back at the studio began to roll the tape they'd been given by a local. Devon watched and shook her head. She turned and walked away. She spared a moment to give a brief wave to the police chief who was holding an impromptu press conference near the dock.

They'd found the body an hour ago and already news crews and reporters were pouring in. Devon kept her head down and kept walking, wanting nothing to do with any of it. She didn't like publicity and didn't want her name attached to this in any way. She spotted Arthur by the local pub, well out of way of the reporters. He was wrapped in a blanket as he sat on the bench outside and was sipping from a glass of amber liquid. A kindly looking woman was stood beside him. He nodded at Devon and beckoned her over. She hurried along towards him.

"Here lass," he said, handing her another glass of the same liquid. "I think you probably need this."

"You poor dear," the woman said. She picked a blanket up from the seat beside Arthur and slung it around Devon's shoulders. "You just sit here and calm down. Terrible thing that's happened, nice young girls like you don't deserve to see that sort of thing. No one does."

Devon smiled and took the blanket and the drink. She settled down beside Arthur and put her laptop on the table, opening the lid and turning it on. Arthur sat and watched.

"I can't believe we found another one," he said eventually as Devon typed away. "How do two people just get murdered and no one notices?"

"Did you know him? Either of them?" Devon asked.

"Nope," Arthur said with a shake of his head. "None of us did, never seen them before in my life. Then again, we get so many strangers through here it's not really a surprise."

"Well from what I saw..." Devon said. She paused. She took a deep breath and continued. "Arthur, it looked just like the other man, the one they found last night. They were both ripped to pieces. They were just found in different places."

"You think it was the same thing?" Arthur asked. "You think it was Nessie?"

"I doubt it," Devon said with a shake of her head. "I looked at the first body. The wounds were definitely made by a blade of some sort. The second one... I'd have to get a closer look but I bet the wounds are similar if not the same."

"Aye, I'd believe that," Arthur said. "I've lived here my whole life, my family's lived here for generations. No matter what people say around here, that creature has never attacked any one, no matter what. Even when the loch was filled with boats she never hurt a fly. Hell, the otters did more damage to people than she ever has."

"I'll bear that in mind..." Devon said absently.

CHAPTER SEVEN

For the next three days, more and more news crews appeared in the small town by Loch Ness. Every time Devon went down to the bar for something to eat or drink it was teeming with camera crews and reporters. It didn't take long for them to realise who she was and what she was there for. The moment she set foot in the bar they would clamour around her, calling out to her and asking questions. Camera flashes would go off in her face, microphones would be shoved under her nose. The questions never stopped and she found it harder and harder to go anywhere without attracting crowds of news crews asking for answers. She wasn't even left alone on the water when she was doing her sonar sweeps.

The local boatmen were happy for the surge in business and every time she went out on the loch in Arthur's little boat it was only a matter of minutes before boats would appear around her and the questions would begin. The shadows of the boats on the sonar and radar played havoc with her readings and she eventually gave up with an apology to Arthur. He was very understanding of course.

"Are you sure there's nothing else we can do lassie?" he asked her after her apology. "I'm sure there's got to be something."

"We can't stop the press," Devon said with a heavy sigh. "It's a hazard of living in a free country. I'll just stay up in my room and dig into the previous sightings or something. I'd feel better about saying that whatever killed those men wasn't Nessie if I had historical proof that she's never attacked someone."

"Och, I can help with that," Arthur said quickly. She looked at him. "Aye! There's dozens of people round here who've seen her, especially the older folks. They don't talk about it much but if you can get rid of these cameras by proving it wasn't Nessie that killed those men, I'm sure that they'll talk to you."

"Really?!" Devon said. "That would be amazing! No one wants to talk to me so far. They all think I'm just going to do whatever McCallum wants me to."

"Well we're all starting to see you're not," Arthur said. "You're doing your job and that's all. I think most of 'em are just glad you're insisting it wasn't Nessie. They don't like the idea of our beloved monster being a killer and you saying she isn't has definitely won you points."

"That's good to know," Devon said with a smile. "When do you think I'll be able to talk to them?"

"Give me a few days," Arthur said. "I'll have to make some visits and get them to come around."

"Ok," Devon said. "I can do that."

She headed back to her room with a spring in her step. As she walked into the hotel she could hear the shouting in the bar of dozens of news crews talking over each other. She peeked around the corner and saw that they were all looking in the opposite direction or wrapped up in their own conversations. She darted across the open lobby and up the stairs. On the first floor landing she gave a sigh of relief when she realised she'd got away clean. Then she continued up the stairs.

The moment she booted her laptop up in her room the instant messenger programme she used started to ring. She hit the answer button and was met with Danny's face.

"Hey boss lady," the girl said happily. "How are things up there? Still crazy?!"

"Like you wouldn't believe," Devon said. She smiled though, her anxiety easing as she saw a familiar face she knew was on her side. "What's up?"

"Same as always," Danny said with a heavy sigh. "I hate to break it to you but I don't think this thing's going to die down any time soon. I've been looking around the internet, me and your minions and there's just so many stories. It's all over mainstream media too."

"Shit," Devon said. "How's McCallum taking it?"

"He's milking it up," Danny said, a sneer on her face. "Yesterday his company released a statement about increased security at the resort that's not even finished and how they're going to be offering packages for people to try and see the monster of the loch. It's ridiculous."

"Of course it is," Devon said. "I've said every time one of those people appeared that it wasn't an animal that did this. Have they even published that?"

"Yup," Danny said. "You're not going to like it but they're saying you're a fraud and a phony. At least the indie networks are. They're focused on how you only seem to ever prove monsters wrong, that that's how you make your money so you're going to say there's no such thing. The bigger networks... they're a little more forgiving and they've got other experts in who agree with what you said. The men weren't killed by animals. I managed to get hold of the autopsy reports, the formal ones, and I've sent them over to you already."

"Thanks," Devon said. "I'm not surprised about all this. I bet McCallum's having a field day."

"Oh he's loving it," Danny said. "I checked the stocks for his company and for the hotel up there... they've tripled in the last twenty four hours alone."

Devon whistled.

"Listen," Danny said, leaning in closely. "I've been scouring the net and searching through old newspaper archives. I have a friend up in Scotland who works at their national archives too. He's transferred everything he could find to do with Loch Ness and monsters on to the computer and he's sending them to me. I'm doing the same here. I know you can't keep going on the water, not with that circus going on. At least with what you've got to read through you might be able to make some headway."

"I hope so," Devon said. She sighed. "I just want to keep looking though. I've got this feeling that there's something going on here, more than a couple of murdered men and a media circus. Did you have a chance to get the sonar readings from the other day analysed?"

"I sent the recordings over to the marine biology department," Danny said. She frowned. "They didn't recognise those shapes at all. They're unlike anything they've ever seen before. I've sent them out further afield, hopefully we'll hear something back. I did get them authenticated though by the IT department and I've put the back-ups in place."

"You're a star," Devon said. "Right, I'll let you get on with your own stuff now, that dissertation won't write itself."

Danny groaned and hung her head down. She let it thump on to the table. Devon laughed at her and closed the messenger program down. Time to get looking into those reports.

CHAPTER EIGHT

The reports all read the same way. Written by different people, at different times in history they all had a common theme. The creature, whatever it was, seemed to be completely passive. All of the descriptions talked about the creature trying to hide, being scared and trying to get away as fast as it could. Devon looked at her notes and frowned. None of it made any sense. The creature was shy and scared, more prone to getting away from humans. So why would it attack? Why would it kill? Why would it savage a human being to the point of almost unrecognisability? She groaned with annoyance and went back to reading the articles and diary entries. There were dozens. A letter in particular kept gripping her attention.

Clara, I swear to you what I am about to write seems impossible, implausible, unreal. But I assure you, from the very depths of my heart, that it is all very real. If I had not experienced this myself I would not have believed it either. But I did, I was there and I saw everything. It is real. The creature in the loch is real, just as Uncle said it was.

We were out on the water in his boat when it happened. Edgar wanted to go fishing and he insisted that the shores of the loch were too shallow. He wanted to catch a large fish, you know how he is, and he claimed that the only way to do so was to sail out into the centre of the lake, where the water was deepest. I accompanied them because I enjoy being on the water. It was a wonderful chance to do some sketching, the landscape here is truly the most beautiful that I have ever seen.

We must have been out there for a good many hours, the sun was beginning to set. I admit that I had dozed off for a short while but I awakened when Edgar began to call out in excite-

ment. *I turned to see him struggling with his fishing pole. He was almost pulled in! But he kept attempting to reel in his catch when suddenly the line changed direction and charged straight at the boat. What happened next was both terrifying and awe-inspiring. It is the single most miraculous experience that I have ever had.*

Edgar's catch came careening towards us. The water was breaking over its fin on the back. Then it went under the boat. It slammed into it and sent the boat rocking. I wasn't prepared for it, I was on my feet, watching Edgar wrestle with the beast when it struck the boat. I was thrown into the water. I began to sink. I cannot swim, as you well know, and my clothes quickly became heavy with the water. I sank faster and faster. I cannot describe how it felt to have those icy waters closing in over my head.

I was sure that I would drown, convinced and I began to pray. Then something, I'm still not sure what, knocked against me, again and again. I looked around but the waters are so dark, so murky, I could not make out a single clear shape, only shadows. I felt something at my feet though, pressing against the soles of my shoes. I realised at that moment that I was getting closer to the surface. It was raising me up!

My head broke the surface of the loch and Edgar instantly grabbed hold of my hair and began to pull. I had come up right beside the boat and in no time at all he had pulled me from the water and into the boat. I coughed up a lot of water but I was alive and I did not care. I looked around for the creature who saved me but I could only see a small shape in the distance. I hope it was the creature for that shape was so very elegant. I have attached a sketch for you to see.

So you see, my dearest Clara, I was saved by the very creature that Uncle called a monster. It is not a monster. It is a kind creature who I believe wants only to be left alone.

Devon picked up the copy of the sketch which had come with the letter. The artist had been truly skilled, the lake was drawn so well that it almost seemed like a photograph. She would have sworn that it was in fact a photograph if it weren't for the fact that she could see the marks of the pencil on the paper. It depicted the shore of the loch, probably drawn from the boat mentioned in the letter. In the very centre a slim shaded shape emerged, a long neck with a small, narrow head on the top. There were more sketches as well, showing a reptilian creature with wide eyes and large nostrils, sharp pointed teeth poking out from the sides of its long snout. Despite the sketched creature's apparent ferocious appearance the artist had somehow gotten in the feeling of shyness and fear, a kindness in the eyes that Devon hadn't realised was even possible for hand drawings.

She reached for the phone beside her bed.

"Hello, it's Dr. Childs," she said once the front desk picked up. "I was wondering if you could get me some string and some tacks? I need to stick things to the walls."

"You ain't sticking no pins in my walls!" the desk clerk cried out. "I'll get you a whiteboard from the school. They're on wheels and two of the lads will bring it up. It'll get them to stop staring at the journos for a while."

"Oh..." Devon said. "Could I have some dry erase markers as well then?"

CHAPTER NINE

An hour later and a gasping Callum and Jack left her room. They'd heaved the white board up all three flights of stairs and it wasn't a small board. It took up almost all of the free space in the room and when they'd first arrived with it, Devon had wondered whether she should ask to be moved. The stern and slightly angry mutterings of the landlady had changed her mind though. She'd ranted about how busy they were and how all of the 'city folk' were demanding obscure drinks and fancy food.

The fact that the landlady had also brought up an entire box of notecards, paper, pens, markers, string, sticky tape and some old newspaper clipping about the monster in the loch had also made her reluctant to request a move. The woman's parting words, in her thick Scottish accent had sealed Devon's decision to get to the bottom of everything.

"You see that you do right by us girly," she'd said. "You prove that there's no monster or that it's not dangerous and I'll be happy. These journalists might be good for business but they're ruining the town I love and I won't have it."

The woman had stared at Devon for a long moment, looking into her eyes and then had nodded before leaving the room. She'd slammed the door behind her as though sealing her words. Devon immediately got to work sticking all of her notes on the white board. She connected the similar events together with string and scribbled notes on the board beside each stickered note.

When she was done the board was a mess of paper and pictures. String crisscrossed the surface and any bare space was filled with her scribblings. It looked like a mess but in Devon's eyes it all made sense.

The monster was not aggressive. In the entire history of sightings it had never once actively attacked any one. Boats had been tipped, people had been shoved but never had it killed anyone.

"Danni," Devon said when she called her assistant. "I think there's more going on than we thought."

"I think you're right boss lady," Danni said. She looked tired, exhausted and her hair, normally buoyant and crazy, was flat and limp. "McCallum's stock has tripled in the last few hours. There are live feeds of the loch on his website and several of the news networks are using them for live video. You should see the number of boats out there."

Devon glanced out of the window and saw that Danni was right. The entire surface of the lake was filled with boats bobbing and bumping into each other.

"It's insane here," she said, turning back to her computer. "I don't even dare leave my room."

"I cannot blame you for that," Danni said. "Your name's everywhere. People know you're up there and you're trying to prove the monster doesn't exist."

"Great," Devon drawled. "Just what I need. As if the locals didn't hate me enough."

"Actually from the quotes they seem to like you," Danni said. "Listen 'That girl (Dr. Childs) is only trying to prove the monster didn't kill anyone. We all know it here and she's the one who says it wasn't Nessie that tore those men up. We believe her and we're glad she's here' then it goes on to talk about your history of proving the existence of monsters isn't true. They all say pretty much the same thing but all the locals seem to be on your side."

"Well that's something," Devon said. "I suppose they'd rather it was a person killing people than the monster. At least a person can be tried and sent to jail. If it was the monster then it would have to be killed. Bang goes their business."

"Yeah, that's what I thought," Danni said. She rubbed at her eyes. "It isn't the monster though. Is it?"

"Definitely not," Devon said firmly. "I saw the bodies with my own eyes. No animal, alive or dead, attacks like that. The wounds were too clean, too precise. It was methodical and exact, like a person did it to cause the quickest death. The rest was just added in afterwards."

Danni nodded and flicked through some more papers.

"Besides," Devon continued. "The monster attacking like this doesn't fit with its behaviour in the past."

"What do you mean?" Danni asked, returning her attention to the conversation.

"Well all my research says it's shy and fearful," Devon said. She turned the screen around to show the board. "I'm copying everything and sending it over to you. You can recreate the board and see for yourself. But I'm sure that this isn't the monster. It never gets aggressive. It only attacks when it feels threatened and never in a lethal manner. It tips boats, knocks people in the water and shoves them away but it doesn't kill people or even break the skin. In the entire history of the Loch Ness Monster sightings there has never once been a serious injury or death from this creature..."

"Wow," Danni said. "Not a single one? That definitely doesn't fit with what's going on. From the way you've described it..."

"It's gentle and afraid," Devon said. "I know. It sounds like a goat or a cow. Only attacking when it has to and then fleeing as quickly as it can. It doesn't want to be seen or caught or even touched. It shoves and runs. That's it. It's the most passive creature I've ever heard of. So why would it attack now?"

"That's the question isn't it?" Danni said. "We've got a few more files to send to you. Ajay's copying them on to the computer and we're emailing them to you. Hard copies are being sent in snail mail. Honestly though.... It sounds kind of like you're buying into the whole Loch Ness Monster is real thing."

"I could be," Devon said with a laugh. "It's the first cryptid I've come across that isn't associated with death and disaster. It'd be nice if this one were real."

"It would..." Danni said. "Doc... don't go native on me."

"I'll do my best," Devon said.

They spent a few more minutes chatting idly while Devon cleared her head. Their conversation finally ended with an order by Devon for Danni to get some sleep and Danni recommending the same thing to her. She was smiling as the conversation ended but when she turned and looked back at the board her smile fell away.

The creature was afraid and passive and shy. So why was it attacking? And why now?

CHAPTER TEN

"Dr. Childs!" McCallum cried out. "It's good to see you in person again."

Devon smiled politely and shook his outstretched hand. McCallum had demanded the meeting, face to face, and she'd been unable to say no. Particularly when the meeting was requested by a large man with an even larger man behind him standing next to a car. They were stood now near the site of the new resort that McCallum was building, the cause of her entire research trip.

"So..." McCallum said. "Do you have any news for me?"

"Only what I've already told you," Devon said. He didn't say a word or react and she continued with a sigh. "The creature, if it's there, isn't dangerous. It has never killed or even injured someone. It actively avoids being seen. It always has."

"Doesn't seem like it at the minute though does it?" McCallum said. "I mean, the monster's torn two people up so far. Who knows how many more could die?"

"Whatever killed those men it was not the monster," Devon said firmly. "And I'm going to keep saying it. I don't know what killed them, what tore them up but it wasn't an animal. I'm worried that no one's listening to that part of the story, they're just going for the exciting bit."

"Well can you blame them?" McCallum said. He started to walk around the perimeter fence and Devon followed him. "Who wants to hear about people killing people when it could be a monster?"

"I thought you didn't believe in Nessie?" Devon said. "It sounds like you do now,"

"Half the journos in town don't believe in Nessie," McCallum said. "They're going with the story anyway though. Why? Because it's exciting. It's dangerous. It's new. It Sells. And that's what matters to the media."

"Sales..." Devon said. "Sales of their reports are going up. Just like your stock. And how many reservations have you got for the resort now? For the resort that hasn't even been fully built yet?"

"More than you could imagine," McCallum said with a sly smile. "I don't know what happened to those men but I'm glad it did. Shame about them of course but still." He started to get excited. "Everyone wants to be here. They want a glimpse of the monster or to see the police find the next body. People are clawing at the bit to get a look. They don't even care that the monster isn't killing people."

"So you know it's fake then?" Devon said. "That Nessie isn't killing anyone even if she does exist."

"Of course it's fake." McCallum said with a sneer. "It's only idiots who think it's real. But those idiots are the ones who'll pay a small fortune to stay at my hotel just for the chance to see Nessie." He laughed. "These idiot yokels killing each other couldn't have come at a better time. We've got pre-bookings, we've got tour requests. Hell the hotel's already on those websites for monster hunters as a place to stay. The money is rolling in and we're all anyone is talking about."

"Jesus," Devon hissed. "You don't even care that people are dying do you?!"

"They're just nobody locals," McCallum said, waving his hand in the air. "No one would have known about them if they hadn't been murdered."

"Oh my god..." Devon said, a light bulb came on in her head. "This is all a scam isn't it? Part of your sales pitch. I'm just a pawn in your little scheme."

"Probably," McCallum drawled. "But you add legitimacy. If even you can't find any proof that the monster doesn't exist or does exist then anyone could find proof. This will be the only hotel where you can possibly see monsters and hunt for them yourself."

"You're scum," Devon snapped. "You're taking advantage of people for something you don't even believe in yourself. You're nothing more than a snake oil salesman."

"Perhaps," McCallum said. He turned to her with a smirk. "But I make the big bucks and you get some of it too. Don't forget that doctor. You took my money, quite happily. You're not much better than I am."

"At least my claims are based in science," Devon hissed, "Yours are nothing more than rumour and hearsay."

She turned and stormed off, not wanting to hear another word from the businessman who had hired her. She stormed through the building site and straight to the car which was still waiting to take her back. Apparently word hadn't reached the driver that she had left early because as soon as she climbed into the back seat he started the engine and drove back to the village.

***

She slammed the car door shut and didn't say a word to the driver. Instead she raced up the front steps and into the entrance hall. She ignored the calls of greeting from the landlady, the shouts for interviews from the journalists. Taking the stairs two at a time she raced up to her room and started to pack up all of her research and belongings. She stared at the whiteboard, the whiteboard that she had spent so many hours setting up and filling with information. Now it was all worthless, nothing more than a means for a man to trick more money out of willing strangers. She reached for the first photograph. Her fingers were inches away. A knock at the door came, tentative and almost so quiet she might have missed it.

"Yes?" she called from the whiteboard. "I don't want to be disturbed."

"Maybe not lassie," the voice of Arthur came from the other side. "But I want to disturb you. You wanted stories about the monster, I've got a story about your monster. But you can't tell a soul what I'm going to tell you."

"There's no point," Devon shouted. She grabbed the door and swung it open. She stared into Arthur's surprised face. "None of this has any point, don't you get that? McCallum never cared about whether the monster was real or not. He just wanted to make it seem like there was a real chance. It's all been a scam. People are dying, I can't find any proof that the monster exists or even existed in the first place and all he cares about is how much money he's making already!"

"It's real to us," Arthur said harshly. He shoved past her and into the room. "Each one of us who lives here believes in some way in the creature of the loch. Maybe not completely but we all believe. McCallum might not care if Nessie is real or not but other people do. You're doing this for them, not McCallum. He's just footing the bill because he's an idiot. He'll get his comeuppance don't you worry."

Devon sighed and slumped down on to the bed. She rested her head in her hands, elbows on her knees and began to cry. The bed dipped beside her as Arthur took a seat and she felt his large hand on her back, awkwardly patting her.

"Here now, what's with all the tears?" he said gently. "You're not the sort of woman to cry at something like this. I know you, you're strong, you're smart. Are you going to let some arsehole like McCallum get you down or are you going to do what you came here to do? Find that monster, one way or another.""

"You're right!" Devon said. She sat up and wiped at her eyes. "I can do this. It's what I do. Who cares if McCallum doesn't believe? I've got no proof that the monster exists but I've got no proof that the monster doesn't exist. And besides, we need to figure out who or what killed those men."

"That's the spirit Lassie," Arthur said, grinning broadly. "Shove it to McCallum and all those arseholes who call you a fraud."

Devon smiled and nodded her head. She looked at Arthur and frowned.

"Didn't you come to tell me a story?" she asked.

"Och, aye," Arthur said. "I almost forgot. I saw the beastie once, when I was seven or eight years old. It saved my life."

CHAPTER ELEVEN

The boat rocked from side to side, ripples spread out from where Arthur kept slamming the stick into the water.

"Come on Nessie," he shouted. "Come on out, let me take a photo of you."

He clutched the stick in one hand, hitting the water with it over and over again. In the other was a camera, the cheapest one he could find and it had still cost him three months' worth of job earnings. Arthur didn't care though, he only wanted a photo of the Loch Ness Monster. Then he could show his friends and everyone else and he'd be rich. His mum and dad wouldn't have to worry about losing the house or not eat much so that he and his brothers and sisters would have enough to eat. They thought that he didn't know, that he was too young to understand but he knew that there was something wrong and now he wanted to fix it. He'd taken all the jobs he could to make some money; collecting eggs, chasing away the birds from the crops, cleaning windows, mowing the lawns and weeding the gardens, delivering papers. Each and every penny that he had earned, he had saved. His parents wouldn't take the money though so he'd decided to do the next best thing. Use it to make more money.

So there he was, on the middle of the loch in the middle of the day. He should have been at church, that's where everyone else was. But he'd pretended to be sick, wrapped himself in his blankets and jumped around so he felt hot to his mother's touch. As soon as they'd all left and he was sure that they were well on their way to church,h Arthur had jumped out of bed and raced to the loch, new camera in hand. There was no one around, not on the loch or at the shore. He had the entire lake to himself and he was sure to catch a glimpse of Nessie, at least long enough to take a photograph.

It seemed though that Nessie didn't want to play. He was sure that he could see her down there in the depths but the water was too murky, a thick deep green, and all he could see were shadows, black moving shapes in the deep. Arthur leaned further forwards, his stomach pressed against the edge of the boat. It rocked for a moment and his stomach lurched with fear. It quickly settled down though and he focused once more on the water.

"Come on Nessie!" he cried out. "Just one photo, so I can help Mam and Da. That's all I want."

He kept hunting, scanning the depths. There was nothing. He threw himself backwards, on to the bottom of the boat and stared up at the sky with a heavy sigh.

"I'm never gonna get it," he said.

The boat rocked in place. There was the sound of an engine far off, getting closer and closer. Arthur sat up on his elbows and looked around. There was a speedboat, one of the ones owned by rich Englishmen who liked to come up for a bit of fishing now and then. It was roaring across the loch, kicking up a wall of water. Arthur's little boat started to rock as the water buffeted it. It was coming right at him. Arthur stood up, trying to keep his balance and waved his arms in the air, shouting. It was no use. The driver of the boat wasn't looking at him, his head was turned to talk to someone behind him. Arthur watched as everything seemed to go into slow motion.

The man reached down and held on to a lever. He pushed it forward. The boat sped up, engine roaring even louder. It came faster and faster across the loch, streaming over the water straight for Arthur in his little wooden boat. Arthur scrambled for the oars, tried to get them into place. His hands wouldn't work, he couldn't move fast enough. The oars refused to go into their slots. The man turned back at the last moment. Arthur caught a glimpse of the surprised 'O' of his mouth as he saw the little boy in the boat at last, the yanking the man did on the wheel. Then he saw only sky.

The speedboat slammed straight into the little wooden boat, bow against bow. Wood cracked and splintered. Arthur was thrown into the air and then fell, down into the docks. A chunk of the wooden boat slammed against his temple as they flew together. He was out cold. Not even the chill of the water woke him when he landed. He fell and fell and fell, drifting down into the loch.

Arthur came to, surrounded by water and unable to breathe. He thrashed. He couldn't tell which way was up. His lungs burned for air. He kicked and kicked only to realise he was sending himself deeper and deeper into the water. He looked around, eyes stinging from the water. He couldn't feel his fingers, his toes. The camera had gone. There were only small shadows on the surface, far above him. All that remained of the little wooden boat. There was no sign of the speedboat. Arthur kicked and reached, trying to get to the surface. He was tiring. His lungs were screaming. His vision was going black, fading out.

Something moved in the green murk around him, a dark shadow. It was coming right for him. Fast. He tried to swim, tried to move. His sodden clothes slowed him. His need for air overwhelmed him. He could only float there as the shape got closer. Then something hit him, bumped against him really and he felt himself rushing through the water, towards the surface. Something was pressed against his front, warm and cold at the same time, smooth and lightly scaled. His head broke the water in a burst of white spray. He gasped for breath. Coughed and emptied his lungs. He kept gasping for breath and collapsed on to whatever was holding him up. He lay there, draped over whatever it was and let his hands rest in the water as he tried to empty his lungs and stomach of loch water. He felt the water moving between his fingers, slipping through faster and faster. He weakly lifted his head, caught a glimpse of grey flesh beneath him before he realised that he was heading towards the shore.

The creature took him to a shaded patch of shoreline, hidden and almost completely surrounded by low hanging trees. It stopped moving when Arthur's feet bumped against the soil and shale. The young boy tried to stand and stumbled. A long neck and small head gently knocked him, strong enough to keep him upright for a moment. Arthur clutched on to the creature's body as he slowly made his way around it, towards the land proper. The creature nudged him gently as he went until he was out of reach. The young boy collapsed, dripping wet, face first into the grass. He looked towards the loch, wanting to thank the creature. But all he saw was its tail flicking in the air as it returned to the depths.

"Thank you Nessie," he gasped out. Then he passed out.

CHAPTER TWELVE

"They found me a few hours later," Arthur said quietly. "My Mam and Da. When they'd come back from church and found me missing they rounded up everyone and started to look. It was almost dark when they finally got around to that side of the loch. They'd thought I'd drowned when they saw the remains of my boat. I was sick for three weeks after that."

"Wow," Devon said quietly.

She had listened to the entire story intently, sat on the edge of the bed as Arthur had described it all.

"I can't imagine how terrifying that must have been for you," Devon said carefully. "Almost drowning like that."

"Oh it was," Arthur said. "The speedboat owner sold his boat after that, never came back. He'd almost killed one of the local kids and he felt guilty for it. That and no one would talk to him or his buddies."

"I can imagine," Devon said. "But... I'm not sure that it really proves anything. I mean... you didn't really get a good look at the thing did you? You said it yourself, you were barely conscious by the time you got to the shore."

"I know what I saw lassie," Arthur said firmly but not unkindly. "I know it sounds strange but Nessie saved my life and took me back to the shore. She left only once she was sure that I wasn't going to drown again, that I was back on dry land. That doesn't sound like something that would kill people now does it?"

"No," Devon said. She sighed. "It doesn't."

"See?" Arthur said. "This is why you should stay. Not for McCallum or yourself. But for Nessie. She needs someone on her side, someone to talk for her. She is not a killer, she is not a monster. She's like any other animal, only getting aggressive when she's cornered or scared. You can understand that can't you?"

"Yeah... yeah I can," Devon said, a small smile gracing her lips. "Ok Arthur. I'm staying. Thank you."

She stood and hugged the boat man tightly.

"Can you do me a favour though?" Arthur asked, pausing at the doorway. "Please don't tell anyone about that story. I never told a soul and I'm afraid what people will do if they know I've actually seen Nessie."

"Of course," Devon said. "You have my word, I won't tell a single person about this."

After she'd shown him out though she wasn't so confident. There was no way that he'd actually been rescued by the creature. It had probably been a dolphin or porpoise, possibly even a small whale that had found its way into the loch from the sea. It wasn't unheard of for marine mammals to come that far inland after all and there were dozens of well documented cases of dolphins and whales protecting humans who had fallen into the water. Arthur had almost drowned after all and he had only been a young boy with Nessie on the brain. The dying and the scared saw what they wanted to see and years of being convinced of his memory had probably made it seem more real.

She sighed and turned back to her boards. Time to put it all back together again.

CHAPTER THIRTEEN

The next morning, she walked into the bar of the hotel, intending to collect her breakfast and instead she was met by uproar. The journalists were all hurriedly chattering away on their phones and scribbling in notebooks, the photographers and camera crews were checking over their gear. Many of the locals were gathered near the bar, talking to each other and looking over at the newcomers with fear and worry. Devon pushed her way through the crowds, keeping her head down but for once none of them paid her any attention.

"What's going on?" she asked Callum who was amongst the group. "Has there been another death?"

"No," Callum said, not even looking at her. "They've called a town meeting and McCallum stepped up and said he wanted to turn it into a press conference. Everyone's freaking out."

"I can see that," Devon said. "What's it about?"

"Nessie probably," Callum said. He scoffed. "Fat lot of good it'll do them. These folks have locked on to the idea of her being a man killer and they're not letting that go any time soon. Not even the mayor will be able to get them out of town."

"You think he wants to?" Jack asked. "This place is rolling in it all of a sudden. Most money we've seen in years. He's not gonna wanna let that all go right now, if ever. Most of the folks round here might not like the journos but they pay good money and a lot of it."

"True," Devon said. "What time's the meeting?"

"Twenty minutes," Callum said. "Over at the school. Want me to take you over? You're gonna want a good seat."

"I think that's an excellent idea," Devon said firmly. "Lead the way."

The school hall wasn't any calmer. There were even more journalists packed into the small room and most of the residents had already claimed seats in the centre of the room, forcing the journalists to jostle for space around the outside edges. The locals were all glaring at the journalists, daring them to come closer. A table had been set up on the stage and Devon could make out the face of McCallum, the police chief and the mayor already having taken their seats.

The police chief waved when he saw her and indicated a seat close to the front. Devon pushed her way through the crowds and saw an empty chair, three rows back from the front with a white board on it. Her hotel landlady was sat beside it and Devon watched, smiling, as a journalist went to sit on the seat. Helen snarled at the man, practically taking his head off. The man beat a hasty retreat and Devon made her way over.

"You found us then lassie?" Helen said when she saw Devon. "Settle down here and enjoy the show."

"Thank you," Devon said.

She removed the board which had her name printed on it and took her seat.

"This should be good," she whispered to Helen as more people shoved their way into the room.

A hush fell over the room as the last few people walked in and took their seats and the Mayor stood up to talk. Devon sat back in her chair and watched intently. Much of her gaze was locked on McCallum, simply trying to figure out what the hotel magnate was doing at the head table of a town meeting.

"Ladies and gentlemen thank you for coming," the Mayor said, his voice booming in the crammed room. "I know that there is a lot of fear and speculation over recent events. I want to inform you all that we are using all of our resources to catch the culprit for these murders. Every effort is being placed on searching the loch and hunting for anything that may shed some light on these tragic events."

Devon glanced around the room. Few of the locals looked convinced but the journalists were all on the edge of their seats or on tip toe, peering over each other to pay attention.

"Mayor is it true that the Loch Ness Monster actually attacked the police divers you sent into the loch?" one young woman called out, Dictaphone at the ready.

"That is not true," the Mayor said firmly. "There was a disturbance within the water but we cannot say for sure what caused it. What we do know is that the disturbance knocked free the second body and our divers were understandably upset by this."

"Do you have the names of the deceased yet?"

"Have any more people gone missing?"

"Will you be searching the loch again?"

"What does the Scottish government say about this?"

The questions kept coming and coming, each more outlandish than the last. The Mayor did his best to answer them but his answers were usually the same; names could not be released, no one else had been reported missing, all available resources were being channelled from multiple sources to find the culprit. Devon smirked as she listened. It was the classic bureaucratic runaround she had seen so often. When the questions started to repeat themselves she seriously considered getting up to leave. Then the Mayor pulled out his ace card.

"Please, please, settle down," he said, as though talking to unruly school children. "Ladies and gentlemen please. I give the floor to Mr. James McCallum, local business owner and hotelier."

"Thank you Mayor," McCallum said, getting to his feet and walking forwards. "I'm very glad that you're giving me this chance to speak. Now. I know that we're all worried. I know that we're all afraid. I know I am and this is not my home. I feel for the people who have made this area their home, the families, the elderly, the workers and business owners who have been born and bred here.

"I am terrified and I don't even live here. I have no ties to this area save that I've chosen to build my latest hotel here. This is a beautiful place with a rich history and some of the warmest, friendliest people that I have ever met. I chose to make this my home from home with my latest hotel because of these people, because of the beauty that surrounds us. I truly believed that I could be happy here and that in time I would come to love it.

"I was wrong though. Two days was all I needed before I fell in love with this place. And when the attacks came I was as distraught as any of the people who have lived here all their lives. I didn't know those men, I had never spoken to them. But many of you had. Many of you had seen them grown from babies into the men that they were. I cannot begin to imagine the pain that you are going through. But I am sorry for it. I wish that you weren't feeling it, truly I do.

"When I chose to build here I wanted to preserve as much as I could of the local way of life. I wanted to create ties in the community that linked the outside world with this town and gave a unique insight into age old traditions that so often got overlooked. I wanted to make people see that this town is more than just the home of the Loch Ness Monster and showcase exactly how amazing it is."

This was met with rumbles of agreement and Devon was horrified to see even Helen smiling and nodding along.

"And this place is amazing."

The locals began to clap. Devon shook her head and rubbed at her temples. She knew that McCallum didn't care, that he was saying whatever he needed to in order to win public favour. And worse, it seemed to be working. Everyone seemed to have forgotten that he had built the hotel that had riled the creature in the loch up, according to them. They had forgotten that he had brought Devon in, the very same doctor who had apparently upset Nessie even more and caused her to take two human lives.

McCallum of course basked in the applause and cheers from the locals and journalists alike. He smiled and waved wildly, pandering to the cameras. Devon felt a cold chill settle in her stomach and the hairs on the back of her neck raised up with foreboding.

"Sadly, that is all being lost," McCallum said. "Fear and paranoia is running rampant. You are all afraid of going out on the loch, the very thing that makes this place so beautiful, with or without Nessie. Two lives have been lost, human lives, local lives. But I say enough. No more will I allow these people who have welcomed me to suffer in pain, no more will I sit back and watch others trying to find the root of the problem. No more will I allow the people that I have chosen to be my community to suffer alone.

"Today I give my word, no more. Two lives have been lost. That is two lives too many. I will no longer sit back and let others do the work. I have the time and the resources to make a significant difference and despite what my investors and other executives say I will help. Because I care about these people. I care about this town. So I am going to call on resources that the local government don't have, using my own money.

"Three hours ago I contacted a group of highly trained former special forces officers. Two hours ago they accepted my monetary offer and agreed to work for me. One hour ago a plane was dispatched to bring them in. I plan to utilise the skills and experiences of these highly trained and highly specialised men to find and hunt and kill the creature that is responsible for these deaths.

"Because it is a beast. Because it is the monster that it has been called. Because it has taken two lives already and will take more if it is not stopped. No more will I sit idly by and do nothing. It is within my means and within my abilities to help. So I will help. The beast dies!"

By the end of his speech McCallum was red faced and spitting with every word. The room erupted into cheers and clapping. Devon looked around in disbelief. Everyone was on board. Journalists were making hurried scribbled notes to themselves. Presenters were clutching mics and talking in the cameras. But the more that she looked around the more Devon realised that maybe not everyone was onboard. Helen was sat beside her, arms crossed over her ample chest. The Police Chief was shaking his head and reading through notes. Other people that Devon recognised from around the village were glaring and shaking free of the grasps of others who wanted them to join in with the celebrations.

"Come on lassie," Helen whispered to Devon. "Let's get away from this circus because it gets any crazier."

Devon nodded and hurriedly followed Helen from the room. She glanced back at the doorway and saw McCallum watching her, even as he smiled and shook hands with the Mayor. The flashing of cameras drew his attention away and Devon turned, rushing to catch up with Helen.

"I have never heard so much crap in my life," Helen said as

they walked back through the now quiet village. "Who does he think he is, coming here and saying he's trying to preserve the local way of life?! We don't need no help with that. We're managing fine on our own."

"I know Helen," Devon said. "He's an arse."

"You said it girl," Helen said. "Snivelling arsehole. He's playing it up for the cameras, I'll tell you. I bet if they'd never come and none of this had ever happened he'd be sat in his fancy office planning how to take up more of our land. That man couldn't give two hoots about this village or anyone in it. All he cares about is making money and looking good."

"Sadly that is the way it is with most businessmen," Devon said. She sighed. "I've seen it time and time again. It's always the same. Unless there's a reason to seem like they care they carry on like they always do."

"Well we'll see how his grand gesture works out," Helen said. "You'll see. It'll go to pot by the end of the week, you mark my words. And we'll keep going and going, just like we always have."

"I know you will," Devon said. She linked her arm through Helen's as they walked. "I'm starting to think nothing can stop you guys when you make your mind up. Hell, things would probably stay the same even in the apocalypse."

"Oh aye, it would!" Helen said. She laughed. "Everyone out there would be eating each other and we'd all just be sat in the pub having a pint and planning a football match."

Devon laughed. Perhaps everything would be ok.

CHAPTER FOURTEEN

By the afternoon the entire village was in chaos, more than even that morning. Helicopters had been flying back and forth with men and equipment for most of the day and a lot of the press had been cleaned out. The village no longer looked like a media circus or a small peaceful holiday town. Instead it resembled a staging post for a military operation. Tents covered the entire docking area at the edge of the loch. Jeeps and sandbags were everywhere and uniformed men patrolled everything. No guns were in sight but Devon doubted that there weren't any. Amongst it all McCallum had strode around like a conquering hero, giving orders and barking commands that were always instantly followed.

"It's insane," Arthur said.

He had joined her on the bench outside the hotel. She'd been sat there most of the afternoon, watching everything as she read through more of the research that Danny had sent over. Helen had kept her readily supplied with tea and cake and had passed on news from other parts of the village which were being taken over by the mercenaries.

"I can honestly say I've never seen anything like it," Devon said. She poured Arthur a cup of tea. "Even when I was investigating the Beast of Dean there was nothing like this. Just a few farmers with guns and dogs."

"If McCallum wasn't here it'd probably be that way," Arthur said. "Then again if McCallum wasn't here there'd be no problem in the first place."

"I don't know if he had anything to do with those deaths but I'm starting to think he did," Devon whispered to Arthur. "It's all too convenient don't you think? People are against him and the hotel. Suddenly two people turn up dead and he steps in like a hero to save the day and everyone loves him."

"Aye, the thought had crossed my mind," Arthur said. "Still lass, I can't see even him having someone killed just to help his ratings go up."

"No, you're right," Devon said. "But he's still taking advantage of the situation and of people's fears. I don't like it. Why can't people see what he's up to?"

"People are scared," Arthur said. "When they're scared they do irrational things and cling to whatever offers the quickest chance of getting them away from the fear. I've seen it before, out on the ocean. Fear does funny things to a person."

"Yeah..." Devon said. She watched McCallum, "Yeah, it does."

"You're gonna talk to him?" Arthur asked as he followed her gaze. "Will he listen do you think?"

"He hasn't so far," Devon admitted. "As far as he's concerned I'm here to boost the idea of his hotel as a monster hunting spot. I'm not an advisor, I'm not an executive. I'm just a professor in need of money who he hired so he could say he was trying to be thorough."

"Try anyway," Arthur said. "You may be a consultant but he'll listen to you I think. Even just a little."

"And if he doesn't?" Devon asked. She paused. "Well, I suppose I could just keep going on at him and annoy him in to listening..."

"Sometimes that can work," Arthur said. "It's how Helen got her husband to buy the hotel here."

"Really?!" Devon asked. She turned to Arthur excitedly and prepared to listen.

Her attention was diverted for a while, listening to the local stories that Arthur was full of and for a little time at least she could forget the politics and fear that were running rampant through the small village and just enjoy her time with a new friend.

CHAPTER FIFTEEN

Night fell and the village was quiet. Everyone who lived there were in their homes and only the mercenaries were left out of doors. Many of them patrolled around the loch, pairs walking together, torches in hand and scanning the water for signs of movement. Radios hissed and squawked from time to time and the low murmur of voices were everywhere. Small buoys floated on the surface of the lake and men huddled together in the tents with eyes locked on computer screens. As she watched and listened, Devon could pick out McCallum's voice, loud above the others.

Curtains flickered in the houses and many of the windows of the hotel were full of people peering through to see what was going on. Devon shook her head and stormed out of the hotel, headed straight for the command tent and McCallum.

"This is too much," she said firmly. McCallum barely glanced at her but she continued anyway. "Seriously! What do you think you're playing at?"

"What am I playing at?" McCallum said coolly as he turned to look at her. "Why, I'm helping the local people to catch a dangerous monster. After all, I may have been the one to rouse it. I should help sort it out shouldn't I?"

"That's not what you're doing at all and we both know it," Devon said. "You're taking advantage of these people and trying to buy their loyalty."

"It's working isn't it?" McCallum said. He smirked. "We've been waiting for hours now and nothing'.s happened. Lures are set, patrols are going around and still all is quiet."

"I've seen the stocks McCallum," Devon said. "I know that your shares are selling like hotcakes since you made your announcement this morning. I know that you're just taking advantage of these people to line your own pockets."

"A fortunate side effect from unfortunate events," McCallum said. He waved his hand at her. "Why don't you make yourself useful and actually do what I hired you for? Go look for signs that the monster's around."

Devon gawked at him for a few moments. Some of the mercenaries glanced between her and McCallum before backing away a few steps. She narrowed her eyes and glared at the hotel magnate.

"Fine," she said harshly. "But I'm doing this to make sure this search is done right, not because you told me to."

She turned and stormed out of the tent, grumbling to herself. She still heard McCallum's parting words though.

"Of course darling. Don't forget to check your payments have gone through as well."

She paused at the entrance to the tent and listened to McCallum's snickers. Some of the mercenaries were chuckling as well. She partially turned her head, not looking at McCallum directly. None of the mercenaries would meet her eye.

"I may be taking your money McCallum," she said quietly. "But I will not jeopardise my career to say what you want me to say. I have a lot more sway in the world than you realise so be careful."

She left. The tent door swung back and forth behind her. She strode through the small camp, searching for the command centre that held all of the monitoring equipment screens. As she searched she allowed a small smirk to take over her face and the sense of satisfaction that she may have given McCallum something to worry about filled her.

The command tent that she had been looking for was clear to

see once she stopped thinking about McCallum and actually started to look for it. Within moments she was inside and taking a seat at some of the monitors, ignoring the protests from the mercenaries who tried to stop her.

"If you have a problem take it up with McCallum," she said, waving her hand at them. "I'm doing what I'm paid to do, looking for a monster. Now go do something else."

The mercenaries grumbled amongst themselves but moved away after a few moments. Devon didn't watch them go, she focused on the screens, looking for any sign of movement.

Hours passed. Nothing happened. Some of the mercenaries began to nod off, one even stretched out on a table beside Devon and started to snore. Devon rubbed at her eyes as she kept watching the monitors. The patrol reports were coming in steadily but there were longer and longer gaps between them. When she had gone outside of the tent for a walk to stretch her legs and wake herself up some more she had noticed that all the windows of the houses were now dark, everyone having finally gone to bed. She'd returned to her seat a little more awake but still bored.

By three in the morning the radio chatter had all but died and very few people were walking around. Devon stared at the monitoring readouts but didn't really see them, falling asleep in her seat with her eyes open. Then a beep came. And another. Then another. They started to come, faster and faster. Shapes were appearing on the screens. She glanced out of the window, towards the loch and saw people rushing around along its bank. Shouts were beginning to sound and she heard the mercenaries around her starting awake and scrambling to gather their gear.

Devon returned her attention to the monitors. There was movement on them. Many shapes, mostly the same size but still large, gathered together, swirling back and forth in formations she had never seen before. They followed behind a larger shape, so large she wasn't sure what she was seeing at first. She looked to the lake. Plumes of water were erupting in the pattern that the shapes on the screen were swimming in. The water swirled and twisted and the faint sounds of splashing reached her ears. Everything around her faded away. There really was something in the loch, something that she had never seen before.

She watched the movement in the water, the swirls and eddies, the water plumes that erupted from time to time. A sense of calmness filled her. The moon came out from behind the clouds, lit up the lake and brought new lake. She gasped and sat there, frozen and fixated on what she was seeing.

Then the spotlights switched on with clicks and booms. The water lit up and dark shapes appeared beneath the surface. The beauty and magic was gone in an instant. A wail came up from the water as the plumes grew higher. It was pained, filled with suffering and Devon's eyes filled with tears as she watched. The mercenaries shouted. A boat roared from the docks towards the lit up spot of water. A spotlight beamed out from its prow. Another wail, filled with panic came up. Devon watched, still frozen as the boat got closer and closer. Guns clicked above the roar of the boat, shouts came over the radios to prepare to fire.

Smaller plumes surrounded the biggest. On the monitor, the smaller shapes swam around and around the large shape. The plumes came more and more often.

"Lock on targets," McCallum's voice said over the radios. "Prepare to fire."

Devon leaned forward in her chair, eyes flicking back and forth between the shapes on the screen and the water plumes. The behaviour seemed familiar, the pattern they were swimming in stirred something in her brain. She kept watching, time seemed to slow down. She couldn't pinpoint why she recognised the formations. Then there was a sudden surge of movement out on the loch, a dark shadow broke the surface before disappearing. It clicked.

"There's babies!" she screamed into a nearby radio. "Don't fire. There are babies there. She's protecting her young. Do. Not. Fire!"

"FIRE!" McCallum shouted over her, drowning her warning out.

There was a burst of gunfire, water jetted up with each pop. A shriek filled the air. Then dozens came. Devon watched from the entrance of the tent, hand at her mouth. Nausea filled her stomach. The water splashed and writhed. All she could see out there was white foam and the flash of the gun muzzles. Then there was silence. The boat engine had cut out. The water grew still. The lights remained fixed on the spot. Something slowly came to the surface, a dark shape. Then a liquid spread over the surface of the lake, something that wasn't water. It spread like oil, dark and thick. The light caught it. It was red.

"Oh no," she murmured. "Oh no, no, no."

She rushed towards the edge of the loch but was stopped by two heavily armed mercenaries. They held her back and more joined them, creating a line between the dock and the now emerging villagers, woken from sleep by the commotion and gunfire.

"What's happened lass?" Arthur asked, suddenly appearing at Devon's side. "What's going on?"

"There were babies," she whispered, eyes still staring at the lake. "There were babies. She was just trying to protect them. But now they're dead. They're all dead."

Arthur gently put an arm around her shoulder and held her tightly. On her other side Helen had appeared and overheard. She gently took Devon's hand in hers and held it tightly.

"Divers prepare to clean up," McCallum said over the radio again.

Devon started, almost dropping it. After everything that had happened she had forgotten that she was still holding it.

"I'd advise against that McCallum," she said into the radio, her voice stronger than she expected. "Your men just killed her young. She's going to be very, very pissed."

"Stay off the air!" McCallum snapped.

Then the radio went silent. Devon stood, sandwiched between Arthur and Helen and surrounded by the villagers. They watched as a second boat moved out to join the first and dark humanoid shapes dropped into the water. Devon realised she was holding her breath as they went in and released after a few moments of nothing happening.

There was a roar. Stark, desperate, angry. It came from somewhere deep within the lake, close to the centre. Something crested the water, a great shape that broke through the surface and sent ripples away from it. It moved towards the divers, quickly, almost too quickly to watch. There were cries on the radio. Shots were fired from the first boat. The creature reached where the divers had gone in and the water grew still again.

Then it erupted. White plumes and sharp waves appeared as whatever was below the surface thrashed. Dark shapes, limbs and equipment flew through the air in all directions. The white water spouts and thrashing surface turned pink with blood. Screams sounded over the radio for only a few minutes. Devon watched the scene with horror. McCallum called out for reports from the divers. There were none. The water went still and

McCallum kept shouting for information. The people at the dock began to talk amongst themselves, their voices low. A burst of movement on the lake again brought gasps of shock and cries of alarm.

It was a diver, the only one left. He threw himself at the first boat and was quickly dragged up. His hand was clutching something tightly but Devon couldn't see what it was.

"They're dead sir," another voice said over the radio. "Mr. McCallum, all of the divers are dead."

"Get back to shore!" McCallum snapped.

"We've got something sir," the voice said. "It looks like a piece of flipper. It's massive sir."

"Bring it to me," he said. "And get me Dr. Childs."

"I'm on my way," Devon said. "Get that thing on ice but do not touch it."

Devon looked at the loch. The blood was still on the surface, showing clearly now in the floodlights. Shapes were beginning to emerge, human arms and legs and bits of torso. The divers, or at least what remained of them. There were no signs of what had killed them.

"Nessie's angry now," Arthur said. "They took her babies and she's not happy about that."

"Of course she's not," Helen said. "She's Scottish, there's nothing scarier than a Scottish mother on the war path."

"Except a 12 foot Scottish monster mother on the war path," Devon said. She pulled free of the two villagers. "I better go and see what they've found. The last thing we need is McCallum doctoring evidence or even having the chance to."

She turned and pushed her way back through the crowd which still hadn't dispersed. She made her way through the camp, brushing past panicked looking mercenaries and damp soldiers. She could hear McCallum before she saw him and walked straight into the tent he was in, ignoring the men that tried to stop her.

"You're all idiots," she snapped. "Give me whatever it is you found and let me go to the morgue."

"Watch your language Dr. Childs," McCallum snapped. "You forget I hold your wages in my hand."

"You forget that I just watched you slaughter a group of innocent babies," Devon said back. "I told you there was more than one out there and you ignored me. You should have captured it, not killed it."

"I gave these people my word I'd kill the monster," McCallum said, "and that's exactly what I've done. Here's the flipper. Figure out what it is so we can tell the media come morning."

"Yes sir," she said, a sneer on her face. "Just don't forget to mention that you fired, completely unprovoked, in full view of civilians, without even knowing what you were shooting at."

"Just go," McCallum said. "I have families to contact."

For a moment, looking at his tired, haggard face Devon almost felt sorry for McCallum.

"Do you think half a mill will be good enough compensation?" he asked one of the other mercenaries.

Just like that the sympathy was gone. Devon snatched the ice cooler that one of the mercenaries handed her and turned to leave.

"Get me answers Dr. Childs," McCallum called after her.

She wanted to flip him the finger but her hands were still full. She settled for walking away without looking back. She kept walking and walking through the camp and out through the village. The crowds were beginning to disperse but no one had yet gone back to their homes. They watched her as she walked by but seeing her face none of them dared to approach. No one that is except Chief McIntyre.

"What's going on lass?" he asked. He matched step with her despite being dressed in a robe and slippers. "What happened out on the loch?"

"They shot and killed something," Devon said, eyes focused on the morgue. "Lots of somethings. Whatever they were, they were babies. Divers were sent in and the mother attacked. I tried to warn them but McCallum ignored me. Again. The divers were all killed apart from one. He brought this up with him. I'm going to find out what it is."

"Need some help Dr. Childs?" the Chief asked.

"I can manage," she said, "You should go back to bed. It's going to be busy tomorrow."

"I doubt any of us'll be getting some sleep after this," McIntyre said. "If you don't mind I'd like to watch you work. Might learn something and even if I don't at least this way you've got an impartial witness overseeing everything."

"True," Devon said. She reached the morgue and nodded at the Chief. "I can see McCallum trying to discredit me after what I've said to him. And threatened him with…. Why don't you go and get dressed and then do me a favour and collect my laptop from my room? I think I'm going to need the help of my assistant back in England."

"Will she even be awake this time of night?" the Chief said in surprise. He glanced at his watch and his eyes widened. "It's four thirty in the morning. Normal people are asleep by now."

"Believe me, Danny is anything but normal," Devon said with a smile. "She'll be up, researching or playing a game. She might even be working on her dissertation. Smaller miracles have happened before."

"Ok lass," he said. "I'll be with you in a few. I'll send the missus over with tea and biscuits for you. You look like you could use them."

Devon put the bag from McCallum's men on the table and pulled a pair of rubber gloves from the box beside her. Pulling out her Dictaphone from her bag she turned it on and set it to record before she put on the gloves. She carefully removed the tape holding the flap of the bag closed and reached inside. Her fingers felt soft cold flesh over hard bone. She pulled the object out and put it on top of the bag. Then she sat back and stared.

"This is Doctor Devon Childs, examining the item found in the loch after McCallum's hunt," she said. "Object has been removed from the bag. At initial examination it appears to be a flipper of some sort, from a large aquatic creature, possibly reptile in origin."

She carefully picked the flipper up and turned it around, examining each and every inch with her eyes. The entire time she kept narrating for the Dictaphone. It was a large flipper but showed none of the wear and tear associated with an animal of that size. There were no old injuries or scratches on the scaled surface. In fact, the flipper appeared to be almost pristine and the skin was still soft and relatively clear.

"There are no parasites or algae attached to the skin of the flipper," she said. "Nothing to indicate that the flipper or the creature it belonged to were in the water for the amount of time usually associated with a creature of this size. I would expect it to have substantial residue on the skin if it were of any particular age. Most animals in water have some form of parasite or algae within their skin by the time they get to be the age usually expected to have a flipper of this size. I am seeing nothing."

She put it down and sighed. She wiped her head with the back of her hand and looked up as the Police Chief returned to the room with her laptop. He set it up for her on the table in front of her and took a seat beside her. He looked at the flipper and put on a pair of gloves of his own. Devon allowed him to handle the flipper, sure that he would be careful with it, his profession making him used to handling delicate items with care. He wouldn't contaminate anything, handling evidence over the years would have made sure of that. While Chief McIntyre examined the flipper, Devon called Danny.

"Doc," Danny cried as soon as she answered. "Are you ok? That thing at the loch is all over the news!"

"I'm fine Danny," Devon said, "I'm here with Chief McIntyre, we're examining something the special forces guys pulled out of the water."

"What happened up there?" she asked, "The news sites are going crazy, the crypto sites are going mad. Everyone's saying it was the Loch Ness Monster."

"It was," Devon said. "She appeared and the soldiers opened fire. Danny.... She had babies with her."

"Oh..." Danny said. "Oh my god. Did you get a good look at them? Do you know what species they are?"

"I don't know," Devon said. She sighed. "It all happened so fast. One minute they were all breathing up near the surface and the next the soldiers just opened fire at anything that moved out there."

"They got away though right?" she asked quickly, "Nessie and the babies were ok?"

"No," Devon said. She wiped away tears that were beginning to fall. "No Danny girl, they didn't get away. I think Nessie did but her babies... they weren't so lucky. They were wiped out."

"Oh my god," Danny said. Devon watched as she raised a

shaking hand to her mouth. "Oh Devon... I'm so sorry."

"I know," Devon said. "It was horrible. I tried to warn them, to alert them but nobody listened. McCallum gave the shoot order right over the top of me. Danny, it was a bloodbath."

"Oh no." Danny said. "Oh Devon. What... how...?"

"Nessie didn't take it well," Devon continued, taking a deep breath to calm herself. "They sent in a dive team to do a sweep, ten men in all. Only one came back out."

"Good for her," Danny said, sounding fierce and ferocious. "What kind of operation is McCallum running up there?! Doesn't he need permits or licenses to hunt something in the water like that? Can he even do that legally?"

"He's got all the paperwork lassie," Chief McIntyre said, putting down the flipper at last. "Everything he's shown says he's allowed to do it. And even if it didn't I doubt that'd stop him. People are scared, men have died. Everyone wants answers and this thing stopped. The mayor would probably let him get away with murder if it stopped any more deaths from happening."

"Well that's exactly what happened," Devon snapped. "But there was one thing. Danny, they pulled this out of the water," she held up the flipper. "I'm going to attach the camera to the computer and send a live recording to you. I want you to record it and then get in touch with some marine biologists with a few stills from it. I want to know what kind of creature this comes from."

"Will do boss lady," Danny said. "Is that from Nessie?"

"I don't think so," Devon said, putting the flipper back down. "It's not big enough to match the size of the thing I saw going for the divers. It's massive, sure, but it just... it doesn't seem to fit with the size of the creature I saw or the amount of time Nessie's apparently been in the loch. It's got none of the usual weathering or time markers you'd expect on the flipper of an animal this size. It'd take years to grow this big, decades even."

"Maybe for the ones we know about," Danny pointed out, "but if you're going for the obvious... maybe they were really big babies..."

Devon froze and stared at the computer screen.

"Danny, you're a genius!" she cried out.

She scrambled around for her paperwork and all of the readings that she had so far. Printouts from sonars, snapshots of the hunt that had been taken and printed by automatic cameras she'd set up.

"Does this mean I get a raise?" Danny asked. "I have had my eye on a new flat."

"Danny if this is right we'll all be getting raises," Devon said. She didn't look up from her paperwork, flipping through sheet after sheet and spread them out on the table beside her. Then she took a closer look at the flipper. "Yes, I thought so. Danny, I'm sending you over digital files of all the readouts I've gathered so far."

"Right Boss," Danny said. "What do you want me to do?"

"Send them over to Dr. Edwards in archaeology," Devon ordered. "Get him and his wife to look at them and give their opinion."

"But Dr. Edwards' wife is a paleontologist," Danny said. "What good is she- ... oh! Oh! Oh oh! Seriously boss lady?! Seriously?"

"I think so," Devon said. "Make sure you get a copy of the flipper image to them as well. If I'm right then they'll have a better idea than Professor Cooper of what we're dealing with."

"Right-o," Danny said. "Do you need me to send you any of Edwards' articles?"

"Yes," Devon said, "that would be best."

Devon ended the call as Danny disappeared to get to work. She turned to Chief McIntyre with a wide smile on her face. He just looked between her, the computer and the flipper with a lost and confused look on his face. Her smile softened to one of understanding.

"Sorry about that," she said. "Danny and I tend to be on the same wave length and forget that other people aren't a lot of the time."

"What does paleontology have to do with this flipper?" McIntyre asked. "I mean, the marine biologist made sense but a paleontologist? Why is that important?"

"Take a look at this flipper," Devon said as she leaned in towards her laptop and typed away. "I mean, really look at it. There's no fur or feathers, which means it's not seal, sea lion or aquatic bird. There are scales which means it doesn't come from a mammal like a dolphin or whale or even one of the shark species. But the scales are smooth and even and lie flat on the skin as well as being all an even colour which means it doesn't belong to a turtle or other sea living reptile we know of."

"So what does it come from?" McIntyre asked.

"I think..." Devon said. "I think that maybe it comes from an animal like this..."

She leaned back and let McIntyre see the screen. On it was an image of a creature with a small head, four wide spade-like flippers, a long graceful neck leading to a large body and a straight cone-like tail that stretched out behind it.

"Plesiosaur," McIntyre read aloud. He jumped and stared at Devon. "You have to be kidding me?"

"I'm afraid not," Devon said. "I'll have to dissect the flipper to be sure but I believe that it comes from a creature very similar to this one."

"But it's a dinosaur!" McIntyre cried. "They're all extinct."

"Maybe not," Devon said. "As I said though, I can't be sure. I'm going to dissect the flipper, take tissue and DNA samples and make sure Doctor Edwards gets a copy of all of my files. Once I get my results back and I've seen the bone structure of the flipper for myself I'll be able to tell for sure whether it is from a plesiosaur or not."

"And if it is...what then?" McIntyre asked. "Are we going to go public?"

"I'm not sure," Devon said, preparing to dissect the flipper. "Until we know for sure what we're dealing with though I think it's best to keep quiet about this. I'll have more information for you soon."

"Ok," McIntyre said. He glanced at his watch. "Well it's getting late... early.... Midday? Whatever. It's well into morning now and I reckon the sun'll be up. If what your friend said was true then I best be getting the boys together to keep the peace. The journos are going to be going crazy."

"That's probably for the best," Devon said, glancing at the police chief. "Dissections like the one I'm about to do are never pretty. You won't want to stick around, believe me."

"Good luck Lassie," the Chief said as he clapped his hand on her shoulder. "Hope you find us some answers."

"So do I," Devon said.

The Police Chief made to leave but when he reached the doorway Devon called out his name. He stopped and looked at her.

"If Nessie is as big as I think she is and last night they killed her babies..." she said quietly. "Well, let's say she's going to be very mad and very dangerous. She's already taken out

McCallum's divers. I think it's probably best we don't piss her off any more than he already has. We don't know much about plesiosaur in general and this is starting to look unlike any sub-species that's been recorded. We have no idea what Nessie's capable of."

"I had the same thought," the Chief said. "Don't worry. I'm keeping everyone off the loch and away from the water's edge. Those who don't listen will be arrested for endangering public safety. Who's to say Nessie won't come crawling out of the loch and devour everyone if someone goes too close?"

"Sneaky," Devon said.

She grinned before she pulled her mask over her face and looked at the flipper again. Chief McIntyre watched as she cut into the flipper then turned and hurried from the room.

CHAPTER SIXTEEN

Three hours later, as the church bell in the town tolled twelve, Devon stared at her computer screen in disbelief. The flipper lay in front of her, almost completely pulled apart with surgical precision. Its bone structure was almost identical to all of the bone structures that she'd seen online of plesiosaur flippers. It was definitely a part of the plesiosaur family though however it was unlike anything that had been found in the fossil records. But the bones weren't fully developed. They were light and thin with no breaks or healing marks like there were on the adult flipper bones. The flipper had come from a baby.

Fury roared through Devon. The special forces had killed a baby, all of the babies. Helpless, unable to defend themselves, they hadn't even realised that they were in danger when they had approached the lures. They'd been curious, shy and inquisitive. Just like any other animal. And their mother had only approached in order to protect them.

Devon packed up her belongings, shoving things away with force. All the recordings were saved and she carefully packaged the flipper away. She handled it with care, like a delicate object and reigned in her anger as she did so. The moment that the flipper was carefully sealed away and safe though she let it all come rushing back.

She stormed from the morgue building, through the village and back to the camp from the previous night. It was all gone. Every tent and supply box had been packed away. The only sign that anything had happened there the night before was the churned up mud and grass. She stood there, staring in disbelief. Then she yanked out her phone and punched in McCallum's number.

"This is James McCallum," his voice said over the phone.

"McCallum! We need to talk," she snapped.

"I can't come to the phone right now, leave me a message and I'll get back to you," his voice continued, cutting her off.

She hung up angrily and stormed around the abandoned campsite, looking for any clues where he might have gone. She kept dialling McCallum's number but her calls all went through to answer phone.

"It's no use lassie," Helen called out after Devon had circled the campsite for the fifth time. She was stood by the pub and Devon walked over. "He's not answering for any one. The mayor tried to talk to him earlier about what happened last night but got ignored as well."

"Unbelievable," Devon spat. "That no good, pile of crap!"

"Aye lass," Helen said. "Come on, let's get you some food. I bet you haven't eaten yet?"

Devon sighed but followed the forceful landlady into the hotel and through to the bar. The smell of cooking food assailed her nose and she realised that she was starving, the pangs in her stomach screaming at her for food. Helen led her over to a table and within moments a bowl of steaming stew was in front of her, complete with crusty bread and rich yellow butter. Devon tucked in and enjoyed every bite. When she was almost finished she realised how quiet it was, how empty the bar was for the first time in days.

"Where are all the journalists?" she asked through a mouthful of vegetables. "Shouldn't they be here?"

"We don't know," Helen said. "They cleared out about half an hour before you started storming around the quay. Didn't say a word where they were going but all got messages on their phones at the same time."

"Helen!" a man cried out. Jeff rushed in from another room with a laptop in hand. "Helen you need to see this. It's all over the internet."

He put the laptop down on the table. And both Devon and Helen crowded around to see the screen. On it was McCallum, stood in front of a white background emblazoned with his company logo. The mayor was beside him and in front of him a lot of the locals were visible, watching and listening.

"Guess we know where everyone is," Devon said. "I wonder what he's going to come out with this time?"

"Somehow I doubt he'll be talking about the divers that died," Helen said, finally sitting down. "Oh, I think he's starting."

Jeff reached forward and turned up the volume as McCallum began his speech.

"Ladies and gentlemen, people of Loch Ness," he said pompously. "I thank you for taking the time to come out today. As you all know these last few weeks have been troubling for us here at Loch Ness. Men have died, good men. They were killed by the monster of the loch. Yesterday I vowed my time and resources to finding and destroying the creature responsible."

Shouts rang out immediately and flashes of lights went off as the journalists fired up.

"Please, save your questions until the end," McCallum said. They all instantly quietened and he continued. "I am pleased to report that just last night, barely twelve hours after I made that promise we found the beast. We were successfully able to contain it and then destroy it. I have managed to free these townsfolk from the curse which had plagued them for so long."

The room erupted into chaos as everyone talked over each other. The locals on screen were all cheering and celebrating with each other, talking loudly. Devon examined the crowd. It was only the people who had supported McCallum the day before, no one who had showed doubt was there. She shook her head. McCallum started to speak again.

"In an ideal world, we would simply have contained the creature," he said. "However this is not an ideal world. Shortly after capturing the beast it attempted to break free and several of my men were injured. In order to maintain the safety of the men in my employment I gave the command to end its life, to spare it any further suffering and to ensure the safety of all involved. I wish it could have been done another way but this was a living creature and as we all know, living creatures have a habit of being unpredictable."

Devon pushed the laptop away as McCallum started to take questions. She sighed and put her head in her hands.

"That son of a bitch," Helen said. "A few injuries my arse. People died. Those poor men in the water died, torn apart by that monster and he's not even mentioned it."

"He also didn't mention that Nessie's still alive," Devon said quietly.

She was met by silence. She looked up to see Jeff and Helen staring at her in shock.

"You don't remember what I said last night Helen?" she asked, "about the babies?"

Helen shook her head.

"It all happened so fast," Helen said, "I was still half asleep. It's a bit of a blur love."

"Makes sense," Devon said. She sighed. "I guess that's why no one's mentioned the truth then." She looked at Jeff and Helen. "This goes no further, ok?"

They both nodded quickly and Jeff squeezed on to a seat beside Helen. They leaned forward and listened intently. Devon leaned in as well.

"The men did shoot and kill something last night," she admitted, "But it wasn't Nessie. It was her babies. They killed her babies. That's why she killed them. She survived, took her revenge and disappeared again, just like she always does. I have a feeling that this isn't the end of it but Nessie is definitely still alive."

"Oh my goodness," Helen said. She sat back and frowned at Devon. "Is that where you've been all day, making sure Nessie's ok?"

"No," Devon said. "I wish. They found something in the water, a piece of flipper. I examined it and figured out that it came from a baby plesiosaur unlike anything we've ever seen before."

"And McCallum's saying he's killed Nessie?" Jeff cried. "We need to tell people!"

"We can't," Devon said with a shrug. "We've got no proof other than the flipper. Any marine biologist who examines it, anyone in the scientific community who tries to look at it now won't tell the truth. Not with McCallum holding the purse strings like he does."

"So what do we do?" Jeff asked.

"We do nothing," Helen snapped. "Dr. Childs is going to sleep. She's been up for hours and I know she didn't sleep last night. You, Jeff, are going to go back to work and not breath a word of this to anyone. Do you understand me?"

She stared at Jeff. He tried to stare her down for a moment but quickly looked away and nodded.

"Helen, I can't go to sleep," Devon said. "I have too much to do."

"Nonsense," Helen said. "Nessie's been avoiding people for years. I think she can manage a few more hours without you helping her. Now go, off to bed with you."

Devon thought for a moment about arguing but one look at Helen's face convinced her not to. She nodded and climbed to her feet. Up the stairs she went, Helen calling that she'd wake her in the morning, and she let herself into her room. It was exactly the way that she had left it. Devon looked at all of the paperwork stuck on the walls, thought about doing a bit more work but the moment she sat down to remove her shoes was the moment that she was struck with a bone deep weariness. She didn't even undress after that, just threw herself back on to the pillows and fell straight into a sleep full of blood and screaming babies.

CHAPTER SEVENTEEN

The next morning Devon decided to take breakfast out on the tables in front of the hotel, watching the loch. It looked completely normal, as though there hadn't been a massacre of children in the waters just a few days ago. She sighed, shook her head and returned to her full English breakfast.

"Good to see you up and about again," Arthur said, appearing beside her as if by magic. "I called for you yesterday afternoon but Helen said you were sleeping and weren't to be disturbed."

"Helen was right," Devon said with a mouthful of toast. "She checked in on me and I didn't even hear a thing."

She'd woken up that morning covered in a blanket with her shoes and bags neatly stored away against the wall near the door. Her entire body had even been rearranged on the bed so that she was more comfortably in the middle. It had to have been Helen's doing.

"I didn't see you yesterday," Arthur said, probing for information in a very unsubtle manner. "Did the hunt upset you that much?"

"No," Devon said quickly. Too quickly. "Well yes. But I was examining the item they pulled from the water just before the divers were killed. I had to figure out where it came from and then send my findings back to England for Danny to pass around. After that Helen pretty much ordered me to bed."

"Aye, that woman's a force of nature," Arthur said. He took a seat beside Devon and leaned in close. "Listen, there's something I think you need to see. It's some footage that I managed to get, not long before the first body showed up. I think it'll help you."

"Really?!" Devon asked. She wiped her mouth and stood up,

throwing the napkin on to the plate. "Let's go then."

Arthur nodded, stood and led her through the village. Right on the outskirts, close to the water's edge they stopped outside a small two bedroom cottage. Arthur led her inside and into the living room. A large tv was in one corner with a high-tech camera plugged into it.

"Hey," Devon said. "Isn't that one of mine?"

"Erm..." Arthur mumbled. He rubbed at the back of his head. "I may have borrowed it lassie and set it up somewhere around the loch. I had this feeling you see, that there was something going on. And it caught something. I was right."

"You stole my camera?" Devon said. "Arthur..."

"I was going to give it back!" he cried. "But then the body was found and I'd fetched it but hadn't had time to watch the video. Then things kept happening and last night, after the attack in the loch I remembered the recording and came to get you."

"That's why you wanted me," Devon said. "Let's see it then."

She took the seat that Arthur indicated and he sat in the armchair beside her.

"I set this up on the opposite bank," he explained as he fast forwarded through hours of darkness. "I'd noticed strange folk round and about as well as movement that weren't animals in the woods near there. So I went over and saw footprints in the mud on the shore. That's when I decided to set this up. Ah, here it is,"

Torches suddenly appeared on the screen, lighting up the darkness but making it hard to see too much of anything. The camera quickly adjusted itself though and Devon spotted two men in dark clothing, clutching torches. Their faces were lit up by the headlights of a vehicle parked just behind them. They were familiar to her somehow.

"The sound's a bit crap," Arthur said. "It was windy and I'd hidden the camera in the middle of a bush. Watch the jeep."

Devon leaned forward and watched as another two men appeared. They were carrying something, something heavy that sagged and dipped in the middle. The two men were also familiar. They juggled their load and the lights of the first two men spilled over it. She sat back and gasped.

"Is that?" she said, not willing to finish her sentence.

"Aye," Arthur said with a nod. "That's the first boy they pulled from the water."

"He's already dead," she said. "And where are all of the injuries?"

Arthur didn't need to reply. Devon watched, speechless as the men dropped the body on the ground and knelt over it. She caught the flash of a knife and saw it cutting into the flesh. She shook her head. She leaned forward again as the four men all took a limb and lifted the body up. They shook it around before throwing it, carelessly tossing it, into the loch. She could hear the splash over the rustling of the leaves.

"They get the other boy too," Arthur said. "Then they cut him up as well."

She watched as the men did just that, repeating exactly what they had done to the first body on the second. She could hear mumbled voices and the words 'McCallum', 'plan' and 'orders'. She watched as they threw him into the water too. They turned around and headed back to the jeep. Their faces were brightly lit for the first time since the recording had begun. Devon cried out as recognition sparked in her mind.

"Pause it!" she shouted. She knelt down in front of the tv and stared at the frozen faces. "I thought I recognised them."

"I thought so too," Arthur said, "I just can't work out how."

"They're special forces," Devon said, sitting back on her heels. "They work for McCallum. No wonder they arrived here so quickly the other day."

"They were already in the area?" Arthur said.

"Exactly," Devon said. "And they're the ones who mutilated and dumped the bodies. I knew Nessie had nothing to do with that."

"So what was the point?" Arthur asked. "Why go to all of that trouble and then shoot Nessie and her babies? Doesn't that defeat the point of all of this?"

"No," Devon said with a shake of her head. "It's genius. But sick. He's even more of a bastard than I thought he was."

"Lass?" Arthur asked.

Devon gave a disbelieving laugh and sat back down in her chair.

"Of course," she said. "It's so obvious."

"Not to me Devon," Arthur said.

"It's all been a marketing scam," Devon said. "Bringing me up here. Setting those bodies up to be found, making them look like they were killed by an animal. Leaking it to the press. I mean, he said it himself, the new resort's the talk of the town, hell the entire world. It's booked solid for weeks and it's not even finished yet." She sat bolt upright. "That sick twisted bastard! He used me!"

"If you're right he's used us all," Arthur said. "But what about the other night? That wasn't a plan, was it?"

"No..." Devon said. "No. It couldn't have been. McCallum sounded just as surprised and scared as the rest of us. He didn't actually think the Loch Ness Monster was real. Hell, he still doesn't. Nothing was actually supposed to happen but he's smart enough to work with a change of plan like that."

"So he tries to fake a Loch Ness Monster," Arthur said slowly, "but ends up bringing out the real one?"

"Of course he did," Devon said. "He had to make everything look convincing. That meant he needed to actually act as though he were luring the monster in. Nothing was supposed to appear. Then when it did he leapt at the chance and ordered the special forces to fire." She stopped. "Oh that bastard! That sick, sick bastard."

"What?" Arthur asked. "What about that press conference earlier though? If he's saying Nessie's dead no one's going to come and look for her are they? His hotel's pretty much ruined now."

"No, I don't think so," Devon said. "He's probably got a plan or something that means in a few weeks Nessie will be sighted again and everyone will come rushing back to see the creature that survived death. It's so wrong."

"And he brought you in to make it all seem more real," Arthur stated. "What are you going to do? Go home?"

"No," Devon said, firm and steady. "I already knew he was just using me. I have a different plan in mind."

Devon spent the next few hours, after talking to Arthur and watching the video, in the hotel bar, sipping at drinks and stewing over what she had discovered. She had known she was being used, she had known that McCallum wasn't being totally honest. But she had still been surprised to discover the depths of his deception. She found herself wondering about the bodies, where they had come from, who the men had been before they were killed, why no one had come forward to claim them. It was just another part of the mystery around what was going on at the loch. Another mystery began to emerge as she sat there in the bar though, listening to the conversations going on around her.

"Did you hear?" one of the regulars said to Helen after a few drinks. "Those special forces blokes set up camps all around the loch."

"Aye," another spoke up. "They're paying good money to camp on my land. They're saying they want to make sure they find all the remains of the creature."

"Bullshit," the first cried out. "I was there the other night, I saw what happened. They didn't kill Nessie, she killed them. She's still out there, they're just making sure no one can get close enough to say otherwise."

"McCallum said they killed her," the second argued. "He put it all over the world."

"He's full of crap," the first man said. "We all know he lies his arse off when he needs to. And right now he needs to. Doesn't want to admit he got a load of men killed without any results."

"I don't know Angus," the second man said. "I saw the blood on the lake the next day. They definitely killed something."

"Probably a bird," Angus said. "They get everywhere. Half my crops get eaten by those pests every year."

After that they started to discuss the problems of birds on the loch and the havoc they caused. Devon blocked them out and turned to her notes. Arthur had sketched her a map of the loch and marked down spots where he'd seen McCallum's men dumping the bodies. It was on the opposite side of the loch, far from where the bodies had been found. They must have somehow drifted all the way around. He really had been crafty about it all. Helen brought her a drink over.

"Helen?" Devon said quietly. "Where on the loch are the men that Angus was talking about? McCallum's special force blokes?"

"The special forces camp?" Helen asked. She saw the map and pointed at a spot on it. "About here I think. Jeff saw another here as well." She pointed at another spot on the map. "There may be more. Want me to ask around love?"

"Please," Devon said with a smile. She marked down the points that Helen had pointed out. "Don't be too obvious though, I don't want McCallum to know I know."

Helen cocked her head to one side and tried to work her head around what Devon had just said. Eventually she nodded and smiled.

"Mum's the word love," Helen said.

She turned and walked away. Devon watched her go. Then her phone beeped. It was a voice mail message. Devon frowned at the screen, she didn't recognise the number that it had come from. She called her answerphone anyway and listened to the message.

"Doctor Childs," a familiar voice said. Devon groaned. "Jim McCallum here. I want you to stay around a little longer and see if you can find out more about what we found in the lake. I know you're not happy with what I've done but it had to be done. We've got results and everything is going great. Once I release your report about what it was that we shot then we'll be world famous and so will you. Keep things up and there'll be an even bigger pay check in your future."

Devon growled and almost deleted the message. She stopped though, her thumb mere millimetres from the relevant button. While he hadn't said anything overly incriminating combined with the information that she already had, she actually had a chance of exposing McCallum for what he was. A lying cheating bastard who used people for his own end. She saved the message. Then she returned to her research. It looked like she was going to be here for even longer.

CHAPTER EIGHTEEN

Rumours kept coming about more camps for the special forces guys over the next few days. Helen helped gather as much information as she could and Arthur kept bringing more detailed descriptions of each one to Devon. Some of the other villagers, the ones who had doubted McCallum and still did, came to Devon and told her what they knew about the camps. Two days after she had seen the footage of the special forces men dumping the bodies into the loch, Devon had a map of the loch that was ringed in red crosses, each one marking the site of a camp. They really had surrounded the entire lake. Word had it as well that they were chasing away anyone who got too close.

There were more rumours as well, rumours of some of the camps being abandoned or completely destroyed. Several villagers shared stories in the bar about seeing several of the man piling in to a car and driving very quickly out of the area. Arthur hadn't been able to confirm those rumours though. He had claimed to have hatched a plan to find out for sure however and he'd borrowed some of her equipment to do it.

"Dr. Childs," Jeff called through her door that afternoon. "Arthur's here to see you again. Says he's got more news."

"That's fine," she said. "Show him up."

Arthur rushed into the room before she'd even finished speaking. His face was alight with excitement and a broad smile. He clutched two of her cameras in his hands.

"We've got it," he said, his voice low but still excited. "We've got more proof."

He shoved the cameras into Devon's hands and sat down on the seat by the window. He looked at her expectantly before she turned and plugged the first camera into the tv she'd had brought to her room.

The screen was dark at first, just a few lights flashing back and forth. Then the camera adjusted and turned on its own night vision filter. There was a camp, tents and jeeps surrounding a circular space in the middle. In the background she could see the splashing of the loch against the shore. Amongst the tents there were people moving around and the occasional flash of a torch from within the nearby trees showed up even more men keeping watch. Everything seemed quiet and she sat for a few minutes just watching the same scene play out, with only slight movement from the men in the camp.

"You're gonna want to fast forward lass," Arthur said, "until the two am mark."

Devon did as Arthur said and fast forwarded the video, pressing play again moments before the clock in the corner of the screen clicked over to two in the morning.

"Ok," Arthur said. "Watch the shoreline."

Devon leaned forwards, her eyes locked on the points of the video where she could see the water lapping against the shore. Everything seemed normal, the same as it had been all night for a few minutes. And then there was a shadow. Something emerged from the water and disappeared into the trees. Devon stopped, paused the video and looked at Arthur.

"Keep watching," he urged her. "Keep watching!"

She pressed play again and kept watching. The shadow re-emerged. There was the crashing of metal, tearing of material, shouts and screaming from the men. The shadow kept moving, dashing between tents. It moved awkwardly, almost as though it were limping or dragging itself along. On one end of the shape a long thin tube dashed from side to side, slamming into anything that got in its way. Men went flying. On the other end was another tube, thicker and shorter. It too whipped from side to side but it was more flexible, with better control. The night vision filter couldn't show it clearly, there were too many lights flashing around, the spotlights that were turned on making the picture blur and the image go out of focus. Everything was white washed.

The crashing and screaming continued though. The shadow moved around. Devon saw the flashing of eyes at one end. She heard car doors slam, screeching brakes and roaring engines. The sounds died down eventually. The screen was still not clear. Devon leaned forward, as though trying to clear the image with just the force of her mind. The creature, for she was sure that it was a creature now, leaned forwards and sniffed at the tattered tents and upturned tables that she had caused. It roared, ferocious, and then let out a bellow that was filled with sadness. It turned and shuffled back to the loch, disappearing into the waters with barely a ripple. The video kept playing, showing only out of focus destruction and the crackling of branches.

"Arthur," Devon said. "Was that...?"

"Aye girl," Arthur interrupted her. "That was Nessie."

"So that's the reason the camps have been clearing out then," she said. "Those men might be special forces but an angry momma monster can still scare the crap out of them."

"They've realised what they've done," Arthur said quietly. "Likely McCallum told them the creature wasn't real so they thought they'd have an easy time of it, pretending to hunt something that wasn't there and sitting on their arses most of the time. Now they realise she's real and she's angry, they're thinking twice."

"Sucks to be them," Devon said. "Do you think any of them will talk to me?"

"Doubt it," Arthur said. "These men have been trained to stay quiet. They might not agree with what they're doing but I bet McCallum's paid them enough that they won't talk."

"Crap," Devon hissed. She sat back with a sigh. "Oh well, at least I've got something to go on. I'll send the video down to Danny, see if she can fix it up at all. She's got a few people who owe her favours."

"Is that a good idea?" Arthur asked. "They could talk, leak it to the press. It'll be that circus all over again and McCallum could bring in some really, really big guns."

Devon sat and looked at Arthur. For the first time she saw how affected he really was by all of this. His face was pale and ashen. His eyes were dull and red-rimmed. He seemed not to have slept for days and there were creases on his skin that hadn't been there when she had first met him.

"You might be right," Devon said. "We'll sit on this for now. The last thing we need is McCallum ordering another attempt to capture the creature. Who knows what he'd do next."

"Man's madder than a bag of pigs," Arthur said.

A knock came at the door. Devon scrambled to turn off the tv and hurried over to the door.

"Who is it?" she called.

"Chief McIntyre," the man on the other side replied. "I'm sorry to disturb you Doctor Childs but there's something we need you to take a look at. I'm afraid there's been some more deaths...."

"I'll be right there," Devon said. She turned to Arthur. "Take that tape and hide it somewhere safe. Try and make a copy if you can and leave it here in my room. Helen will let you in if you ask." She paused and thought. "And see if she'll take a copy as well, keep it in the hotel safe. I can't see any nosy reporters or

McCallum's men getting past her."

"Aye," Arthur said with a firm nod. "Helen's a terrifying ban-shee of a lady but she's a good woman, she'll help us if we need it."

"Good," Devon said. "Now, I better go and see what sort of death and destruction I've got to deal with this time."

She grabbed her bag and made to leave the room. As she passed through the doorway Arthur called after her.

"Tenner says it's something to do with Nessie?"

"I'm not taking that bet," she called back. "Not on your life."

By the time she arrived at the crime scene, having gotten a ride in the front of a police car for the first time in her life she was glad that she hadn't. It was another of the special forces camps, a little smaller than the one on the video and much clos-er to the loch. The destruction was massive though, parts of the camp were strewn across the field it had been made in. She could see forensics officers with tape measures measuring how far some of the pieces had travelled.

"This isn't pretty Dr. Childs," McIntyre said as he led her through the destruction. "I'll understand if you want to walk away. But I think you really do need to see this."

"I think I'll manage," Devon said confidently.

She wasn't so sure though once she entered one of the white tents dotted around the area. Even the coroner looked a little green and as Devon looked over the masked and suited man's shoulder she soon realised why. The bodies barely resembled bodies any more. As far as she could tell there were at least three men there, possibly more. They had essentially been flat-tened. Bits of bones poked through skin and the entire mass was covered in a thin red film. Intestines had burst through stomachs, smearing their contents over everything and the entire tent reeked with the stench of half-digested food.

"I think you can see why we needed you," the Chief said, a handkerchief muffling his voice. "Short of a bulldozer or steam roller I can't think of anything man-made that could have done this."

"That's because it wasn't a person or machine who did this," Devon said.

She knelt down beside the mass of bodies. She gently poked around with a gloved hand and a pair of forceps. She hummed in satisfaction as she pulled out a scale, holding it up to the light for the investigators to photograph.

"I've seen something similar to this before," she said, getting back to her feet. "In Africa. I was hunting for a Massai creature they believed was kidnapping tourists and children. Just down from where we were camped one night was a bunch of American teenagers, sightseeing and bush camping. Their guide tried to tell them to keep it down in the evening but they decided they wanted to go swimming at the river. Unfortunately for them it was home to about thirty hippos, one a massive three ton bull. He didn't take kindly to naked humans invading his territory and he ran three of them down before they could escape. He rolled on top of them, mashing them together. They looked very similar to this after he was done."

"A hippo?" Chief McIntyre said. "You think a hippo did this?"

"No," Devon said. "But something big, and heavy did. I'm not sure what though."

McIntyre nodded and beckoned for her to leave the tent. She followed him out and back across the crime scene, to his car. Once inside he sighed but didn't turn the engine on.

"Tell me honestly Devon," he said. "Was this Nessie?"

"It depends," she said.

"On what?" he said.

"On who I'm talking to," Devon said. "Chief McIntyre who tries to do the right thing by everyone, or Chief McIntyre who wants to keep the Mayor happy."

"Does it matter?" he asked.

She turned and looked at him, right in the eye. He sighed and rested his head on his arms, dangling over the steering wheel.

"You're talking to Doug," he said quietly after the silence had stretched out for long minutes. "You're talking to the man who lives in this town and wants to keep people safe but also thinks that McCallum's up to something and isn't telling us."

Devon looked at him again, staring at him. Finally, she nodded.

"Ok. It is Nessie," she said. "I told you that McCallum had her babies killed. Well now she's getting revenge."

"I thought so," McIntyre said. "We've got camps like this all around the loch. Some of the bodies are worse, completely torn apart and then mushed up. Some it looks like the special forces guys got out before she could do more than hurt them a little. And some of the camps we've been getting reports of being completely abandoned, like they just got up and left in the middle of the night. They didn't even take their weapons with them, just got in the cars and scarpered."

"That doesn't surprise me," Devon said. "You might have been joking about Nessie coming out and devouring anyone who gets too close but it looks like she might be doing just that. At least to the special forces guys."

"I hate it when I'm right," McIntyre said. "So what do we do? I can't exactly come out and say there's a giant dinosaur killing everyone around the loch and McCallum didn't actually kill it.

There'd be a bloody riot."

"Keep it quiet for now?" Devon suggested with a shrug. "I'm not great with cover-ups, I deal with facts and truths. For now though I think we need to keep the dinosaur aspect quiet. The media's leaving us alone for now, it'd be nice to keep it that way."

"McCallum's got to pay for this, lass," McIntyre said firmly. "He's brought this all on us."

"I know and he will," Devon said firmly. "I'll deal with him. He's got to be sweating as it is, all of his special forces mercenaries running off like this, not to mention even more deaths. I'm building a case against him. I'll see if I can get him to say anything incriminating."

"He isn't avoiding you?" he asked. "I've tried to call him several times and I've even sent people to his office and home. All to no answer."

"He's avoiding me all right," Devon said. "But he wants me on side. I'll just have to bite the bullet and pander to his ego a bit first I think. He should at least talk to me for this."

"Just be careful Devon," he said. "You're a nice lassie and a lot of us round here have grown quite fond of you. Hell, we've seen more of Arthur in these last few weeks than we have in the last few years alone. And he's smiling!"

Devon laughed.

"I'll be careful," she said. "I'm fond of you lot too. And I know how to take care of myself, don't you worry."

"I don't doubt it for a second," McIntyre said with a smile.

He finally started the engine and they drove back to the town.

CHAPTER NINETEEN

"The results say it's plesiosaur," Danny said with a shake of her head. "I can't believe it. Analysis puts it at between three and six months old. Archie did some of his fancy reconstruction stuff and came up with an estimate of its current size and probable growth rate."

"That's great Danny," Devon said. "Really great. But it doesn't get us any closer to bringing McCallum down. We can show all the data and prove it was just a baby that they killed but he'll just bring out lawyers to make himself look good and they'll argue that we're only showing half the science or something."

Danny sighed. Devon watched her for a moment as she spun in her chair, thinking, before she turned back to the results that Danny had sent over. They'd been having their conversation over the computers for the last hour or so and it was beginning to wear.

"Look, there's nothing we can do unless we get McCallum to catch himself in a lie," Devon said firmly. "There's no point going over and over this anymore, we're just going in circles. I'm just going to have to play nice and speak to him tomorrow. He's already booked an appointment with me."

"Those camp attacks have him spooked?" Danny asked.

"Yeah," Devon said. "Wouldn't they spook you? According to the gossip half of the men McCallum have hired are missing after running away in the night. And it's not just the camps that have been attacked that are losing people. A lot of the guys are getting out now, before they get killed or hurt in the middle of the night."

"So he's got you looking at the bodies again?" Danny said. "Just like last time. Think he'll actually listen to you though?"

"Unlikely," Devon said. She sighed and rubbed her eyes. "But he might. He's losing the men he's hired and word's spreading that Nessie might not be as dead as he claimed. He's going to want to save face as quickly as he can I think. Chief McIntyre told his men to let slip that I'd seen the bodies, to make sure that word got to McCallum, or at least that's what Jeff's told me. It can't be coincidence that those rumours got out and I finally get an appointment."

"He's kind of transparent when you think about it," Danny said. "Not exactly the business genius you'd expect from his reputation."

"Well my reputation is for disproving monsters," Devon pointed out. "Here I am trying to prove the Loch Ness Monster exists and protect her from being revealed to the world."

"Kind of goes against the grain a bit," Danny said. "You sure you want to keep this all quiet?"

"Yes!" Devon said, quickly and firmly. "I've seen this place, I know the people. I saw what happened the last time the media were here and she's already lost one set of babies. I don't want to bring that down on this place again."

Danny thought for a moment and nodded. They talked for a little longer about random things, double checked information and eventually hung up. Devon looked through the notes that Danny had sent her, all of the files and documents. Her eyes hurt from staring at the screen. She needed to print them off. And she knew just the woman to ask.

CHAPTER TWENTY

McCallum found Devon the next day in the small lounge no

one really went into at the hotel. She was tucked into a corner near a window, looking out over the loch from the comfort of a wing backed chair. The table in front of her was covered in sheets of paper and the odd empty tea cup. She had a notebook on her lap and a pen in her hand as well as another in her hair. Her mouth moved as she read the words on the papers aloud but with no sound and scribbled down notes on the pages of her notebook. McCallum cleared his throat and she jumped.

"Mr. McCallum," she said, unfolding herself from her chair and reaching out a hand. "So sorry, I got a bit wrapped up in my research."

"Still looking into Nessie I see?" he said, nodding at the paper work. He took a seat opposite where Devon had been sitting. "I told everyone Nessie was dead."

"With all due respect James," Devon said, "we both know that's not true. I know you only killed her babies and you know that she's been attacking the camps where your mercenaries are staying. We might not see eye to eye but right now, at this moment, we want the same thing. We want Nessie to go back to being a quiet peaceful creature that rarely gets seen....albeit for different reasons."

"You're still sure that she's real?" McCallum said. "Even after everything that's happened?"

"I'm even more sure that she's real," Devon said confidently. "I've seen the proof for myself and so have your men. That's why they're all disappearing, isn't it?"

McCallum's jaw clenched and the knuckles of his fingers went white as he clutched at the arm of the chair. He took a deep breath and tried to plaster a smile on to his face. It looked more like a grimace.

"How did you hear about that?" he asked through clenched

teeth.

"This is a small town Mr. McCallum," Devon said, leaning forwards in her chair. "People talk and stories travel fast. But we need to stop those stories before they get out in to the wider world. Don't we?"

"Yes," McCallum snapped. "Yes we do. But right now I'm more interested in the bodies of my men, specifically what you've seen when you've examined them."

"Heard about that did you?" Devon said with a smirk.

"Small town, juicy gossip," McCallum said, throwing her own words back at her. "Just tell me what you know."

"This time it was definitely an animal attack," Devon said confidently. "The bodies were crushed together, rolled on and trampled by something heavy. Injuries and bruising suggests that they were knocked over and brought to the ground first, before anything else. Then they were trampled."

"How can you be sure it was an animal that did this?" he asked.

"Tracks," she said. "This time there were tracks, leading in and out of the water and there were no tracks or marks left by a vehicle that could have done that to people. And I've seen that method of attack before, in Africa by a bull hippopotamus. Whatever attacked them tracked their scent through the water and used the cover of darkness to get out of the water and attack them."

"How could it see?" McCallum asked. "As far as I heard it was pitch black the nights of the attacks."

"The clue is in the eyes," Devon said. She pulled out a collection of shots of eyes and laid it in front of him. "Marine animals tend to have eyes that suit their environment. In this case it would have large pupils for seeing in the dark waters of the loch.

Given the scarcity of sightings I'd wager that she spends a lot of her time down there, in the deeps. She may possibly even have a cave that leads to an air pocket where she rests. It would explain why she's never seen on the surface."

"That's our next step then," McCallum said firmly. "We are going to sort this out. We're going to find where this monster is living and get rid of her finally. I will not have any more of those mercenaries running out on me. And I will not be branded a liar."

"Of course," Devon said calmly. "I think we have the right equipment here already, I'll just need a few hours to check through everything and set it all up."

"You're co-operating this time?" McCallum asked.

"Of course," Devon said. "We both want to find Nessie and to be honest you were right. She was becoming a danger to everyone. She's killed too many people and it's time to stop her. Going to her home is actually the smartest thing to do when hunting a creature, I'm not surprised at all that you knew that."

"It is?" McCallum asked, frowning. Then he straightened up. "Of course it is. Go to their home, flush them out or just kill them there. Best way to get rid of dangerous pests. Like with rats."

"Exactly," Devon said. "But I'm a little worried that we might not have all of the right equipment. Should I give you a list of anything else we'll need when I find it?"

"Of course," McCallum said. "I'll certainly be able to get it for you."

"I thought so," Devon said with a warm smile. She stood and began to gather her things. "Would you like me to call you once I have everything ready or would a text be more convenient? I would hate to interrupt something important."

"Don't worry about it," McCallum said, standing up as well. "This is very important right now and I've cleared my schedule. Just send me a message with the equipment you might need and then call me when we're all ready to go out on the loch."

"Of course," she said with a nod.

McCallum looked at her, smiled and turned away. He walked out of the lounge without looking back. As soon as he was out of sight Helen stepped out from behind a curtain near the doorway, cup of tea in hand and a smile on her face.

"You're wasted monster hunting lassie," she said, walking over. "I have never seen anything like that."

"Momma did say I should have been an actress," Devon said, flicking her hair over her shoulder. "But the call of animals was too strong and I couldn't resist!"

"I was a little worried you'd gone too far," Helen said. "Did you actually bat your eyes at him or did it just sound that way?"

Devon grinned.

"I did... not," she said. "But at least I've got what I need. Hopefully this will be what we're hoping for. I'll find Nessie, McCallum will try and kill her, we'll record it all and stop him and you'll all get left alone."

"And if it doesn't work?" Helen asked.

"Then we spend an entire day and night floating around on the loch," Devon said with a shrug. "If she stays hidden that might be even better. Then we'll be able to keep her existence a secret and everyone will put the stories of the special forces guys down as PTSD or a marketing scam by McCallum."

"Now I know why you wanted Arthur on the boat," Helen said. "At least you'll have one friendly face on board."

"That and he's a sneaky bastard," Devon said with a grin, "I swear, half the time you don't even realise he's there until he says something."

Arthur and Devon waited at the dock. Arthur looked out over the still, calm water. Devon had her back to the water and her eyes were locked on the approach road, scanning it for signs of someone coming.

"I don't like it," he muttered, "I really don't like this, girl."

"I know," Devon said, glancing at him quickly. "I'm not a big fan of this either but the faster we get this done with, the sooner Nessie gets left alone to mourn."

"He needs to pay," Arthur said. She could practically feel him vibrating with anger. "He needs to pay for what he's done."

"He will, don't you worry," Devon said. She spotted something and stood up straighter. "Here they come. Put on your happy face Arthur."

Arthur grumbled but he turned around anyway to face the oncoming car. He didn't look happy but then again Devon had rarely seen him smile except for when he had talked about Nessie. The car pulled to a stop and only four people climbed out. Three of them were special forces and the final one was McCallum.

"Dr. Childs!" he cried out. "Glad to hear we're good to go."

"Is this all the men you're bringing?" Devon asked, an eyebrow raised. "I thought you'd bring more."

"I was going to..." McCallum said, walking towards them, "But I decided against them. Is this the way to the boat? Everything's set up, yes?"

He didn't wait for an answer. He walked straight past Devon and Arthur and down the jetty towards the only boat that was bobbing at the dock. The others had all been cleared out for the failed stake out that had ended in death and no one had brought them back. The special forces men followed after McCallum.

"What's the betting all of his other men are gone?" Devon whispered.

"I'm not even going to take that bet," Arthur said firmly. "Momma didn't raise a fool. Now let's get aboard before that idiot breaks something or sinks my damn boat."

Arthur stomped down the jetty and to his boat, muttering under his breath the entire way. Devon followed behind, smiling and shaking her head at him. She paused at the plank leading to his boat and looked out over the water. She shivered. The hairs on the back of her neck stood on end. She scanned the water. There was something out there, watching her. She was sure of it.

"Come on Doc," McCallum said, startling her. "Let's get this show on the road."

He disappeared below decks as quickly as he had appeared, leaving Devon by herself again. She spared one last glance out over the water, looked back towards the town and then climbed on board Arthur's boat.

CHAPTER TWENTY-ONE

Out in the middle of the loch McCallum and Devon were sat in front of the sonar monitor, staring at the display. The special forces men were sat at the back of the boat, fiddling with weapons Devon hadn't even seen them bring onboard as well as checking their diving gear. Arthur was at the helm, eyes fixed on the water and saying nothing as usual. They'd been sailing back and forth for what felt like days. Really it was only hours but being around McCallum made time stretch for Devon. He had constantly talked away about nothing and everything that didn't interest her and also spent a good portion of the time droning on about the increase in sales since his press conference. All the time the sonar readings had been quietly pinging away with each pass around and no unusual readings had popped up. McCallum had launched into a tirade about planning permissions and protesters when Devon finally got up and walked away. He still kept talking to himself, even while she went and stood beside Arthur.

"Do you think the soldier guys would notice if we threw him overboard?" she murmured to Arthur.

"Probably not," he said. "But Nessie might eat him and I don't want to do that to her. He'd just make her sick."

"True..." she said quietly. "I just wish -"

"Doctor Childs!" McCallum shouted, cutting her off. "Come quick! We've got something."

Devon rushed over and looked at the monitor. There was definitely something there. She leaned in closer.

"Looks like a cave entrance," she murmured. She shouted to Arthur, "can you circle back around for a few minutes?! I think we might be on to something."

"Boys, get ready to go," McCallum ordered.

"What?!" Devon said even as the special forces men began to put on their diving gear. "You can't send them in there. You don't even know what's down there."

"I'm paying them, I can send them wherever I like," McCallum said. "I want this creature found and destroyed."

Devon took a step back. There had been so much hatred and venom in McCallum's voice. His face had been twisted with rage and turned red. It wasn't a good look for him and it made the hairs on the back of her neck stand on end. One of the special forces soldiers brushed past Devon and fiddled with another monitor, one she hadn't even noticed until that point. Suddenly it was on, screen bright and filled with three separate images. All were of the boat from different angles.

"We're not going to be caught unawares this time," McCallum said firmly. "We're going to see that bitch coming."

"You got cameras," Devon said.

McCallum glared at her and turned his attention back to the screen. Devon watched him for a few minutes, watched his hired soldiers preparing themselves and then turned and went back to Arthur.

"I don't like this," she murmured. "I don't like this at all."

"Me neither," Arthur said. "Something's going on. Those men are packing some serious fire power."

Devon looked over at them. They were already preparing to dive into the water. She spotted several guns on their waist belts, ones that were specifically designed to fire underwater. Her stomach began to churn in time with the rocking of the boat. She wanted to say something, wanted to stop them. But she was frozen, locked in place and she could only watch as the men dropped over the side of the boat and into the dark waters of the loch. The splash seemed to release her and she rushed over to the monitor, eyes scanning the feed outs from the cameras in the water.

"So much for seeing her coming," Devon said. "It's like swimming in soup."

"Just keep the sonar going," McCallum snapped. "I'll watch my men."

Devon glanced over at Arthur who shrugged. She looked at the camera monitor one last time then focused on the sonar screen. She had a duty after all, a duty to keep the men in the water and everyone on the boat safe. It had been her idea to go out looking for Nessie. She had been the one to make McCallum aware that Nessie wasn't gone, that she was still very much alive. The sonar pinged. It pinged again. The camera screens showed nothing, just the divers.

"Keep going," McCallum ordered in to the walkie talkie he now held. "Keep going down, you're clear."

They kept going down and the sonar kept pinging, showing a large shape near the silhouettes of the three divers. McCallum tapped something on the computer and readouts of the divers' vital signs suddenly appeared on the images from the cameras. Devon stared at him for a moment then leaned in close to the screen, peering to try and see through the murk. She was sure that she had seen a shadow, something moving out in the dark behind one of the divers. The sonar kept pinging.

"Something's there!" McCallum snapped into the walkie talkie. "Wilkins, behind you."

One of the screens showed a blur of movement through the water, bubbles filling the screen. Then it settled and all the three people on the boat could see was the deep green of the water and the light dancing through, making patterns in the gloom.

"There, on your two o clock," McCallum said.

Devon had seen it, a flicker of movement, a shadow, something moving so quickly that she almost wasn't sure that she'd seen anything at all. A gasp from Arthur beside her told her she had. The other two screens were showing just water with an occasional glimpse of fish or the other divers. Suddenly one of the screens was filled with bubbles, a hint of red, spinning water and a dark shape. Then it went black and the vital signs cut out.

"What..." McCallum said. "What just happened?"

"He's gone," Devon said, her voice faltering. "He's just... gone."

McCallum just blinked at the monitor and leaned in closer.

"There!" he shouted, pointing at one of the other screens. "I see her! Get ready to fire, take her out!"

"She's just defending herself!" Devon said. "We've come to her home and attacked her, what did you expect to happen?"

"She's going down," McCallum snarled. He raised the walkie talkie to his mouth. "Prepare to fire.

Devon quickly scanned the images and gave a small cry when she saw a dark shape coming straight at the screen of one of the remaining divers. She screamed as she saw it all on the monitor of the remaining diver, as the dark shape zoomed in to the second diver, massive crushing jaws clamped around the man's midriff, an explosion of blood and the two severed halves slowly floating down and out of sight. Devon stumbled back and half turned. She buried her face in Arthur's chest and he gently held her to him, stroking her hair.

"Oh my god!" McCallum said. "Oh my god, oh my god, oh my god."

Devon slowly turned back to the monitors and watched the only remaining working screen. There was a wide open mouth, teeth everywhere and a deep black hole of the creature's throat.

Then the camera showed only static and the life signs vanished.

"They're dead," Devon said shakily. "They're all dead."

"We need to leave, lass," Arthur said quietly, pulling away from her. "We need to get out of here."

"No!" McCallum snarled. "She's going down. What can she do to us that she hasn't done already? She's been a problem for long enough. She's a relic that should be dead, it's time to make that happen."

"She was protecting herself!" Devon said. She stepped away from Arthur and towards McCallum. "We've come here, killed her babies and now we're hunting her. She's going to fight back. We need to leave!"

"No way," McCallum said, shaking his arm free of her grasp. "I'm calling the media. They'll help me hunt her down."

He stepped away from Devon and Arthur who were heading towards him, trying to calm him down. He kept stepping backwards, away from them and towards the railing of the boat.

"McCallum, we have to leave," Devon said. "Like, right now!"

He held out a hand, warding her off and with the free hand scrambled in his clothes for his phone. He pushed Devon away as she got too close and pulled his phone free. He started to dial. Suddenly something knocked against the boat with a heavy thump and they rocked madly for a moment. The phone in McCallum's hand slipped free, he waved his arms wildly to try and catch it but it kept slipping free until eventually it tumbled through the air and over the railing, falling into the water with a small splash. McCallum spun, put his hands on the railing and stared at where the phone had disappeared.

"Get me a phone!" he screamed, turning around.

His eyes were wide and his face was red, twisted and lined as he snarled and glared at Devon and Arthur.

"We're going to get the media, get the police and get the fucking army out here," he snarled as he paced back and forth. "We're going to take out this bitch, get rid of her once and for all. I'll ram her with the fucking boat if I have to."

He headed towards the helm. Arthur reached out to stop him but McCallum shook him off. The crazed businessman grabbed a hold of the helm when something hit the boat again and they rocked from side to side. McCallum barely kept himself upright, Devon had to grab hold of a nearby post to stay on her feet and years of experience helped Arthur stay steady on his feet. They were showered with water from above and there was a great splash.

Devon looked over to the side of the boat and saw a column of grey flesh, rising from the surface of the loch, up into the air. She followed it upwards, higher and higher until she came to its head. It was long, narrow with a rounded snout. Its eyes were wide, round and blinking slowly. There was sadness there, a deep, all-consuming sadness. It tipped its head back, opened its teeth filled mouth and roared angrily. The three all stood there, frozen in place as they stared up at the creature. Devon's heart was in her throat, her chest pounding so hard she could hear it in her ears. It was Nessie. They were finally face to face with the Loch Ness Monster.

As Devon kept looking at the monster the fear started to leave her. It lowered its head and kept looking at them. This wasn't a monster, this was a creature from the beginning of time. It was something that had never been seen before, had never shown itself. It had the deepest, darkest green eyes that Devon had ever seen on an animal. At first glance Nessie's skin was completely brown but as the creature leaned over them she saw that there were patterns of greys and greens on its flesh as well and even a few patches of orange. Devon wanted to just reach out and touch it, touch her. Instead she looked it in the eye. The creature kept lowering and lowering its head until it was snout to nose with Arthur.

Devon watched, holding her breath. Nessie sniffed at Arthur and then gently nudged at his chest with her snout, rubbing against him. He closed his eyes and smiled, reaching up with a steady hand to stroke Nessie's head. Then Nessie pulled back and her head swiveled towards Devon. She moved closer and sniffed at Devon's clothing, bumping the woman gently with her nose. Devon watched with her mouth open, looking Nessie right in the eye. Nessie pulled back and just stared at Devon, head tilted to one side. Then she moved on.

McCallum flinched as Nessie came to him and sniffed at his clothing. She smelled him for longer than the others, going back once or twice more, sniffing at him furiously. Devon could hear each deep breath clearly. Nessie reared back, eyes locked on McCallum. She roared. There was so much anguish in that roar, so much hatred. Devon realised what was going on. She could smell the special agents on his flesh, on his clothes. She could smell the gunpowder and gun oil, the blood of her babies. Devon couldn't react as Nessie struck, her neck bending and darting forward like a pouncing snake.

McCallum barely had time to scream before Nessie's jaws clamped down on his throat. He reached up, tried to claw at her skin. It was no good. She was too big, too strong. She pulled and pulled, dragging him off and into the water.

Devon came back to herself then. She scrambled for her phone and rushed over to the side. A few quick swipes on the screen and a tap and she thought she'd captured the perfect picture of Nessie. She looked. When she looked at the picture she had taken though her heart fell a little. All there was of the image was a big black blob and loads of water. She couldn't use the picture. It proved nothing. She looked over at Arthur, he was smiling sadly at the spot where Nessie had vanished beneath the waves. Then it hit Devon. She had seen Nessie, she had seen the Loch Ness Monster. Monsters were real.

The tears prickled at her eyes. This whole time... she'd thought they weren't real, that they didn't exist, that they were just the result of a poorly educated working class in history and people trying to exploit fear. But now she knew otherwise. Now she knew that they weren't lies, that they weren't made up, that they were real. Monsters were real.

Arthur put his arm around her and held her close as they slowly steered the boat away from the scene, back to port.

CHAPTER TWENTY-TWO

The crowds of journalists were back the next day. Devon and Arthur sat on the benches in front of the hotel, watching as they crowded around Police Chief McIntyre and the mayor. The two men were speaking clearly and loudly, straining to be heard over the chatter of the journalists.

"As of yet we have no information as to the location of James McCallum," the police chief said. "What is clear however is that the special forces soldiers that he hired under the guise of hunting down and tracking the Loch Ness Monster were in fact the ones responsible for the deaths and mutilations of the bodies that were found within the loch in the recent months. Video footage was recently handed in that shows several of the men mutilating the bodies that were discovered and dumping them within the loch."

Devon's eyebrows shot up. She hadn't known that. She turned around and stared at Arthur. The older man wouldn't meet her eyes. She kept looking. He glanced at her, sighed and looked at the table.

"Arthur..." she said. "What did you do...?"

"I leaked the video to McIntyre," he mumbled. "I handed it over before we left with McCallum and told him to look at it if McCallum never turned up again or if we all went missing. I guess he looked at it anyway."

"Aye," Helen said, suddenly appearing at their side. "I spoke to Cousin Glennis, she lives two counties over. Apparently, a bunch of those special forces blokes were hiding in her town. The police swooped in yesterday and arrested the lot of them. Charged them with murder and mutilation of bodies and everything."

"Hopefully they'll get some hard time for that," Devon said. "Not that it'll be a problem for those guys. They're trained killers after all."

"I heard some of them are making deals," Helen whispered. "Ratting out on McCallum so they can get a leaner sentence. They're not happy they're getting in so much trouble for this, apparently they were only following orders."

"Isn't that what the Nazis said?" Devon said. She sighed. "Well, at least there's no evidence of Nessie being real now. Everyone knows that McCallum faked it all and made everything up. You all get your peace and quiet and she gets left alone at last. At least for the next few decades anyway."

A car beeped near the hotel. Devon looked over and smiled.

"Here's my ride," she said, getting to her feet and gathering her bags together. "I promise to come back and visit. And you just need to keep an eye on Nessie for me."

Arthur climbed to his feet and hugged her tightly before turning and collecting her bags. Helen hugged Devon while he took them to the car and helped the cabbie load them up.

"Now remember girl," Helen said firmly, "don't go trusting everyone you meet. Never work with worthless millionaires and always have some faith in the seemingly impossible."

Devon laughed and hugged Helen again. She turned to the cab and gave a soft cry as she saw all of the people she had met during her time in the village lined up on the other side of the taxi, waiting to say goodbye. Each of them gave her a tight hug or a warm handshake and wished her well. Some shoved their email addresses into her hand and promised to be in touch. She eventually climbed into her taxi and waved at them all as she finally drove away. They stood there, in a crowd, receding into the distance as Devon kept waving out of the back window.

These were the people she'd helped, the people who'd become her friends while she had been there.

It was only when they disappeared around a bend and out of sight that Devon finally turned around and settled into her seat. It was going to be a long ride to the airport and an even longer flight. With McCallum gone she was stuck with regular planes this time. At least he'd paid her before Nessie had dragged him off to the depths. That was something.

EPILOGUE

At her flat it felt like nothing had changed. Everything was exactly as she had left it: a complete mess with clothes and paperwork everywhere. But she felt changed, utterly changed. She took out the picture that she'd taken of Nessie, printed in the airport's Boots shop, and tacked it to the fridge. She smiled. Nessie was real. Who knew how many other monsters were still in existence. Her smile grew wider. Then her phone rang. She didn't recognise the number.

"Doctor Devon Childs speaking," she said quickly.

"Devon!" a cheery voice said, his accent a mix of English and Russian. "Good to speak to you. How are you, old girl?"

"Sergei?" Devon asked, "Sergei Jones, is that you?"

"Of course," Sergei said. "I wasn't sure I'd reach you. Thought you might still be all locked up in Scotland and under investigation because of the McCallum thing!"

"No," Devon said, laughing. "They thought about it but considering I had no knowledge of what they were actually up to and McCallum's notes said he was using me as a beard they figured I didn't really have a reason to kill him. After all, I was just doing my job up there."

"Well I'm glad to hear it," Sergei said. "How have you been otherwise?"

"Sergei..." Devon said, a hint of warning in her voice. "I haven't heard from you in three years. I know you're not just calling for a chit chat."

"You caught me," he said. He sighed. "Truth is we're having a bit of trouble over here. The Russians brought me in as an independent surveyor on some land formations where they want to build a new road, you know, making sure it stays up and stuff.

The land's pretty sturdy and should hold up well, real high quality granite-"

"Sergei!" Devon said, cutting him off. "You like rocks, I get it. Time to focus on the issue though."

"Oh right, yeah," he said. "Well anyway. They're bringing in the workmen and I'm staying with the builders, just in case they come across a different rock type. But they're having a bit of an issue and now the workers are on strike. It's a major problem and no amount of money is making these guys work again."

"Get new workers?" Devon said. "I don't understand what this has to do with me?"

"Devon, if it was as simple as that it'd already be done." Sergei said, "Russia's a country that runs on money. They've taken capitalism to a whole new level here. But it's not about the money. Devon, these guys are scared. Even the foreman's scared and so are my bosses even though they won't admit it. No one will work on this road until we get this sorted."

"What's scaring them?" Devon asked. "Something tells me it's not a bear."

"It's a Menk," Sergei said. "More and more of the workers have being seeing it near the work site and the word's spreading. They're saying the Menk doesn't want the road built and there have been a few accidents and over-night equipment damage. They're blaming the Menk."

"So you want me to come and prove it's fake?" Devon asked. "I don't know Sergei."

"I'm just asking you to come and look around," Sergei said. He suddenly sounded exhausted. "We're up on Dyatlov Pass, in Russia. It's practically in the middle of nowhere apart from one small town and it's surrounded by forest. The army's talking about firebombing the entire area. Devon, the town would be destroyed, if not by the fire then by the destruction of the forest. Their entire lives are hunting and trapping and woodwork in those woods. With it gone they wouldn't last long."

"Menk.... Isn't that a Bigfoot?" Devon asked. "They think a Bigfoot's trying to stop the road being built...?"

"Yeah," Sergei said. "Devon... I think it's real. I think I've seen it. I need you to come and help, in any way you can."

Devon glanced at the picture. Someone thought Bigfoot was real. They said they'd seen it. She'd heard that before. And Nessie had been real, one of the most iconic cryptids in the world was real. Who knew how many others were too.

"Sergei," she said. A smile spread across her face. "You need to get to Moscow. I'm coming to Russia."

ABOUT THE AUTHOR

Daniel Marc Chant is an author of strange fiction. His passion for H. P. Lovecraft & the films of John Carpenter inspired him to produce intense, cinematic stories with a sinister edge.

Daniel launched his début "Burning House" in 2015, swiftly following with the Lovecraft-inspired "Maldición." His most recent books "Mr. Robespierre", "Aimee Bancroft and "The Singularity Storm" and "Into Fear" have garnered universal praise.

He has featured in the anthology collections "Cthulhu Lies Dreaming" from Ghostwoods Books, "Death By Chocolate" from KnightsWatch Press, "VS." from Shadow Work Publishing and "Bah! Humbug!" from Matt Shaw Publishing, and "The Stars at My Door" from April Moon Books.

Daniel also created "The Black Room Manuscripts" a charity horror anthology and is a founder of UK independent genre publisher The Sinister Horror Company.

You can find him amongst the nameless ones on twitter@danielmarcchant, and at facebook/danielmarcchant.

He doesn't bite.

Much.

CHECK OUT OTHER GREAT DEEP SEA THRILLERS

MEGA
by Jake Bible

There is something in the deep. Something large. Something hungry. Something prehistoric.
And Team Grendel must find it, fight it, and kill it.
Kinsey Thorne, the first female US Navy SEAL candidate has hit rock bottom. Having washed out of the Navy, she turned to every drink and drug she could get her hands on. Until her father and cousins, all ex-Navy SEALS themselves, offer her a way back into the life: as part of a private, elite combat Team being put together to find and hunt down an impossible monster in the Indian Ocean. Kinsey has a second chance, but can she live through it?

THE BLACK
by Paul E Cooley

Under 30,000 feet of water, the exploration rig Leaguer has discovered an oil field larger than Saudi Arabia, with oil so sweet and pure, nations would go to war for the rights to it. But as the team starts drilling exploration well after exploration well in their race to claim the sweet crude, a deep rumbling beneath the ocean floor shakes them all to their core. Something has been living in the oil and it's about to give birth to the greatest threat humanity has ever seen.

"The Black" is a techno/horror-thriller that puts the horror and action of movies such as Leviathan and The Thing right into readers' hands. Ocean exploration will never be the same."

CHECK OUT OTHER GREAT
DEEP SEA THRILLERS

PREDATOR X
by C.J Waller

When deep level oil fracking uncovers a vast subterranean sea, a crack team of cavers and scientists are sent down to investigate. Upon their arrival, they disappear without a trace. A second team, including sedimentologist Dr Megan Stoker, are ordered to seek out Alpha Team and report back their findings. But Alpha team are nowhere to be found – instead, they are faced with something unexpected in the depths. Something ancient. Something huge. Something dangerous. Predator X

DEAD BAIT
by Tim Curran

A husband hell-bent on revenge hunts a Wereshark...A Russian mail order bride with a fishy secret...Crabs with a collective consciousness...A vampire who transforms into a Candiru...Zombie piranha...Bait that will have you crawling out of your skin and more. Drawing on horror, humor with a helping of dark fantasy and a touch of deviance, these 19 contemporary stories pay homage to the monsters that lurk in the murky waters of our imaginations. If you thought it was safe to go back in the water...Think Again!

CHECK OUT OTHER GREAT DEEP SEA THRILLERS

LAMPREYS
by Alan Spencer

A secret government tactical team is sent to perform a clean sweep of a private research installation. Horrible atrocities lurk within the abandoned corridors. Mutated sea creatures with insane killing abilities are waiting to suck the blood and meat from their prey.

Unemployed college professor Conrad Garfield is forced to assist and is soon separated from the team. Alone and afraid, Conrad must use his wits to battle mutated lampreys, infected scientists and go head-to-head with the biggest monstrosity of all.

Can Conrad survive, or will the deadly monsters suck the very life from his body?

DEEP DEVOTION
by M.C. Norris

Rising from the depths, a mind-bending monster unleashes a wave of terror across the American heartland. Kate Browning, a Kansas City EMT confronts her paralyzing fear of water when she traces the source of a deadly parasitic affliction to the Gulf of Mexico. Cooperating with a marine biologist, she travels to Florida in an effort to save the life of one very special patient, but the source of the epidemic happens to be the nest of a terrifying monster, one that last rose from the depths to annihilate the lost continent of Atlantis.

Leviathan, destroyer, devoted lifemate and parent, the abomination is not going to take the extermination of its brood well.

www.ingramcontent.com/pod-product-compliance
Lightning Source LLC
Chambersburg PA
CBHW051955170626
46808CB00007B/2635